C. L. EASTON

STRANGERS OF THE TOWN

Strangers of the Town

Copyright © 2022 by C L Easton

Cover Design: Black Pirate Book Cover

Publisher: Black Rose Publishing

Ebook ISBN: 978-1-7782968-2-6

Paperback ISBN: 978-1-7782968-3-3

May you never run out of battery life on your vibrators.

NOTE FROM THE AUTOR

This book is written in Canadian English

This is the conclusion from the first book. Strangers of the Night.

Take warning this is a dark romance. Our three gentlemen all share the same lady, without choosing in the end.

It includes:
Bondage, Impact play, Anal Sex, Double Penetration, Torture of people, Handling of Feces, Blood, Gore, Mention of Abuse.

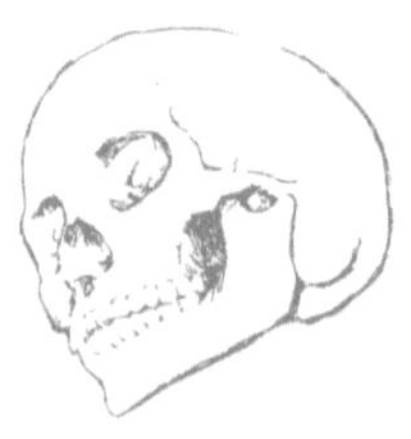

PLAYLIST

AIN'T NO REST FOR THE WICKED- CAGE THE ELEPHANT
CASOLINE- HALSEY
WICHED AS THEY COME- CRMNL
ARSONIST'S LULLABYE- HOZIER
BURN IT- FEVER 333
FUEL- METALLICA
THE RED- CHEVELLE
HOW I COULD JUST KILL A MAN- RAGE AGAINST THE MACHINE
PEOPLE ARE STRANGE- THE DOORS
.INTOODEEP.- DEAD POET SOCIETY
TGIF- K.FLY, TOM MORELLO

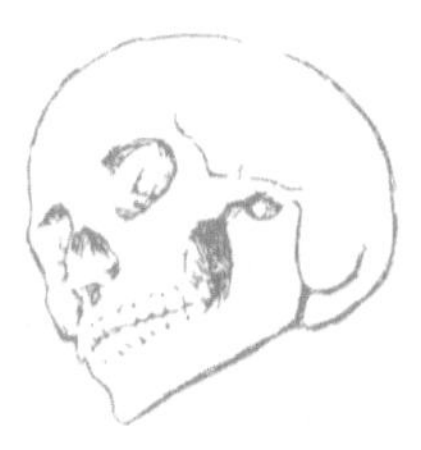

1

DORIAN

My eyes must be lying to me because these men in front of me are not responsible for anything. This Conrad fuck thinks he's caught the grave digger. Little does he know he only saw the ones that were looking out for her. Where we failed, they came through. I can't let them die because of us.

"I'll see that they are properly looked after," I told Henry, "it's technically mine—our job, after all." I gesture between the guys.

Conrad gives me a screwed-up look, I pretty much took the candy away from the baby, and he's pissed about it. The tension rolls off him.

"I suppose that is why I made you all the enforcers, isn't it? I can't be taking away your jobs now, can I. Very well, call me when the job is finished." He nods for Conrad to follow, leaving us alone.

"What the hell is going on?" Cole demands.

Nyx walks over, pulling the cloth from both professors' mouths. While they cough, he explains.

"Catalina's bag is in the corner of the room." He points to the far corner of the room. I turn to look, and he's right. I see her satchel walking over. I bend down and dig through it. I am trying to find anything that will let us know where she is. All I see are snacks, sanitizer, wipes, some other random girl products and her phone.

Which is dead.

"Great, so no clues. Where the hell would she be? How long has it been?"

Professor Davis groans. "I gave her the job earlier tonight. We talked about another job opportunity. I wanted to check up on her because of her hand, and I became worried when she didn't answer. We went to go check on her."

"That's when we found her missing, then the next thing we know, were both hit over the head and waking up in this room," Professor Adam told us.

Great, so no one knows where the fuck she is. "There wasn't anything to hint at where she is?" Nyx questioned them.

They shake their heads.

Cole punches the wall yelling, "Fuck." Rubbing his eyes, he turns to us. "We need to try to find her, retrace her steps or something, the longer she's gone."

He doesn't finish his sentence; we all are thinking the same thing: the longer she's gone, the more time whoever has her can torture her or worse.

"What about them? How are we going to get them out of here and produce bodies for Henry?"

Cole looks at me and smirks. "Guess we're going to have to channel our inner Wednesday. How do you know which ones to dig up?" He looks back at Professor Davis.

"I usually look in the newspaper for the obituaries, then wait until the funeral to see where they are buried. It's not rocket science or anything."

Huh, I figured it was a lot more work than that, but this way makes more sense and is more straightforward.

"But she didn't finish her jobs tonight," Professor Davis said.

"What you mean is, we can use two bodies in the cemetery."

"Jesus Christ Nyx, yes. Does he have to spell it out for you?" Cole snaps, losing his patience.

"Sorry," he muttered.

We need to work together, or it's going to turn to shit; I get that we're all under a lot of pressure, but it's not doing her any good. I try to ignore all the arguing that's going on and try to figure out a plan. If we do successfully dig up these bodies and somehow sneak them into the warehouse, then what? Can you even beat up a dead body? We are so far out of our element. I'm thankful that we watched Catalina dig up that one body. I'm sure we have this in the bag, but It's still a process either way.

As we leave the warehouse, we bump into Freddy.

"What are you boys doing sneaking around here?"

"Freddy, you didn't see us. You got that?" Cole emphasized. "We have shit to do, and we can't involve anyone. We trust you, old man."

Freddy gives us a nod. "I ain't seen shit. Have a good night, boys."

That's one thing I love about him. He'll do anything for us, and I don't think he fully trusts Henry either. I'm not sure why he's still in the gang.

The drive to the cemetery goes by faster than I hoped for. With directions from Davis, we find the van. Everything that we need is inside.

"The question remains, how the fuck are we going to drive this thing into the compound?" Nyx finally asks the question that I've been thinking about.

Cole ponders for a minute. "We'll tell Henry it's the new delivery van only if we get caught. We'll have to get to the compound in the morning. It should work."

I look at him. "And if it doesn't."

"I'm not sure, to be honest."

We headed towards the grave that Cat had started, and everything was as she had left it when we arrived. Perhaps we'll stumble upon a clue here. Whoever took her had to leave something behind. No one is that stealthy. Except we find nothing, just the grave. It doesn't look like there was even a struggle. I have so many questions. Did he sneak up on her? Maybe she ran, and he caught up with her elsewhere? Either way, we need to find her.

"Hurry, this gives me bad mojo. Bodies are meant to be resting. What we're about to be doing will give us bad karma." Nyx looks down at the grave, staring at the body, and a shiver jolts off his body. He was always a sensitive soul.

Cole scoffs. "You're worried about karma? We just killed how many people? But this." He points downwards. "Is bad mojo. Get off that horse of yours. Grab the hook and get down there."

I save Nyx from heading down there and don't mind this sort of thing. Besides, I watched Cat do it, so I feel confident enough. Jumping down into a grave is the weirdest thing I've ever done.

"I can't believe half pint does this for a job. She can barely see over this thing." I strap the hooks under the arms.

"Her job is pretty interesting, isn't it." Cole waits for me to finish before he can haul the body up.

I whistle, letting him know I'm finished. The body slides out of the coffin with a thud, up the dirt, and then I hear the crinkling sound of the body bag. I climb out of the hole and see Nyx zipping up the bag.

"One down, one more to go," he grunts as he hauls it over his shoulder, walking back to the van.

"This time, we'll have to dig, speaking of digging. Where's the shovel?"

That gets us to look around; all her gear is usually in one pile. I shake my head when I don't see it. I reach for my phone and flick the flashlight on, lighting up our surroundings. I walk away to the east of the site. Maybe she took it or threw it. Honestly, I'm grasping at straws. If some punk kids had come, I'm positive they wouldn't have taken a shovel. I'm sure they would've done something with the body. What I don't understand is why, when Conrad picked up the professor's why, he never refilled the grave in again. This whole digging-up bodies was the reason Henry was in a tizzy in the first place, so why leave it open?

"Yo, over here," Cole yelled opposite the side of the grave.

I hustle over to him, and he's bending down, picking up the shovel. We're a reasonable distance away from both the grave and the van.

"What do you think?"

"Either she tried to run, or she used it as a weapon." He looks it over, not finding any blood. We both relax a little. "We need her back, D." I can hear the desperation in his voice. We're all going to go crazy if we don't find her.

We're halfway through digging and haven't exchanged a single word. We switch off every half hour, and the only thing that goes through my head is that Cat does this alone, and she's half my size. I still can't imagine how she can do this more than once some nights.

"How far down do we go again?" Cole asked, wiping sweat off his forehead.

"Till you hit the coffin, I'm guessing." I shrug. "The other one wasn't very deep."

"I'm just hoping this plan works, or all this is for nothing."

I would have to agree with him. If Henry suspects anything, we're fucked. Before I can think more, the shovel hits the coffin. Cole looks up at me, shallows hard.

"Fuck, now I gotta open it."

"Man, the fuck up, you are a member of the Soul Stealers. You torture people, remember." That's the most admirable pep talk I'll ever give.

"Crowbar, let's get this over with."

The drive back to the warehouse has me nervous. It's pushing dawn, and if we're lucky, Henry will still be asleep and be oblivious to what's about to happen. Nyx pulls the van around the back, parking at the doors that lead to the torture room. Climbing out, I stand guard while Cole heads inside. He's going to bring out Davis and Adams while we move both bodies in. Then we'll make it look like we killed and tortured them. Pray it'll be enough, and no one will see the difference. We'll have to pay special attention to their faces, that's my only worry.

The doors open again, and Davis comes limping out.

"You're going to need blood. Dead bodies don't produce," he reminds me.

Ah, shit. Sorta overlooked that, didn't we? "Now what? We don't have time to head somewhere else."

"Check the van. See what you got in there. We might be able to help." Adams says from behind me.

I raise an eyebrow questioningly. "I'm sorry, you might be able to help. How?"

Adams chuckles. "Well, my body was full of blood last time I checked. What about you, Davis?"

"Mm-hm. Red River is a flowing."

I go to say something but come up empty. After everything they've been through, they still want to go through more. Unbelievable. Nyx climbs in the back, digging through all the totes and trying to find something we could use. Except this van is meant for the dead and not the living. What we need is a miracle. Nyx holds up a knife. I look over at them and smile. They jerk their head no, quickly.

"That'll be a no, Nyx."

"Damn. Too bad she didn't have this on her tonight." He tosses it back in the tote and climbs out of the van. "I can't find anything in there. Unless we slice and dice something. We're fucked." He turns to Davis and Adam, raising an eyebrow.

"No, Nyx," Cole says from the doorway. "Get the bodies inside, and we'll figure something out. We can find something inside. You two in the van."

Trying to do things sneakily in a quiet building is hard. Every little sound is heightened. I swear Henry will hear us from his fuckin' shack up the road. I throw a body on the chair, and if you're wondering.

Both bodies are male.

So, our plan will work, and yes, we get the *pleasure* of stripping them naked.

"I'll go and find something we can use. You two strip them and get them tied to the chairs. I don't care what you do to make them look abused." Only Cole would leave us with the shitty jobs.

"Dickhead, who put him in charge again?"

I can't help it. My lips pull into a slow smile. "We did. Cole's technically older."

"Pfft, he's older by two months. So, he's hardly one to give orders."

"No, but you know how he likes to have control and likes to boss everyone around."

We busy ourselves prepping the bodies, waiting for Cole to return. We strip them off their clothes and get them in position. I look at the table with all the tools. I reach for the blowtorch, lighting it up.

Here's to hoping dead flesh doesn't smell like living flesh.

I was wrong. The dead smell is so much worse. Especially when they have chemicals in their bodies. Nyx and I nearly barfed all over the place. All I did was go around their wrists and ankles. I had to make it look like they struggled in their restraints some. Cole chose this moment to walk in.

"Oh, sweet fuck. What is that?" He covers his nose with his shirt.

Nyx points to the bodies, then to the blow torch still in my hand. He places a finger over his lips, tilting his head to the side. He swallows. "He... um... burnt their flesh." He exhales, then walks to the outside doors, opening them a crack to grab some fresh air.

"You sick sonofabitch. I found this." He holds up a syringe. "It'll have to work. This place is empty for emergency shit."

"I guess they'll have to play rock, paper, scissors."

"Unless you torch them some more, then we just add some blood here and there. That should do it. Snap a picture or two. It should keep Henry satisfied."

That's true. It's Conrad who might want to see the bodies. He rubs me off like a fuckin' creep.

We spent the next few hours getting the bodies situated for the photos. Adams ended up drawing the short straw. He didn't seem to care, more relieved than anything because his nightmare was almost over. To be honest, I can't wait till it's over as well. Then, we can focus on Catalina.

I knew we shouldn't have let her go.

2

CATALINA

"You're a worthless whore, Catalina. You're going to mount to nothing." My mother spits in my face. All I wanted to do was go to the school dance, and I didn't think it was too much to ask for. Everyone else gets to go, so why can't I?

"Are you listening to me, girl? Or do I have to get your brothers involved?"

I shake my head. "N-no, mother. I'm listening, I swear." My voice was shaking. My nerves are on edge every time she's around. One wrong move and I'm off to see my brothers, and it's her go to move. I just have to play nice with her. But I want to go to this dance. I don't ask for much, but I want this one thing.

"Please, can I go? I'll only go for an hour, I swear." I look up at her. Her green eyes burned into my violet eyes. Her jaw clenched like madness.

That's where I made my mistake. I looked into her eyes. Not only does she hate me, but she also hates my violet eyes. She says it's what makes me a whore. It'll bring the men in because it's my fault that I was born with them. Before I can move, her hand collides with my cheek. Heat explodes the entire way up my face. I grab the side of my face, keeping my tears at bay. If I dare cry around her, it'll only get worse.

"Don't ever ask for shit. Get to your room. I don't want to see you until I'm ready." Her voice holds a savage edge.

I scramble up the stairs, and the oldest son greets me at the top of the stairs. I freeze, and my body physically shuts down. Fear clawed its way through me. His lips twisted to the side, sneering at me. His dark, empty eyes stare into mine like daggers.

"I heard you were causing grief with Momma. This better not be true."

I felt a lump at the back of my throat. All I could do was shake my head mutely.

"I doubt you know what's expected of you."

My blood runs cold. "Please, no. I promise never to do it again." Lips were trembling around every word. When the rest of the sons appear, it makes the air in my lungs vanish. My entire body shakes, and sweat builds up on my forehead while they stare at me. I gingerly wipe it away with a trembling hand.

A hand clamps down on my wrist, dragging me the rest of the way to my bedroom. Please, no, not the closet. I can't go another round of the closet. Every time I was in there, they left me *longer and longer. I fear this will be bad. The way all the sons are looking at me. I get tossed into my room, and as soon as they all cram inside, they slam the door closed, sealing my fate. I clamp my eyes closed when the first fist meets my face.*

I wake sweaty and wheezing. I haven't had a dream like that in forever. Not since I moved out of that house. I thought I was past all that, so what brought them back? I have no idea. All I know is I'm probably late for class. Rolling my shoulder around, my breastbone cracks, reminding me how sore I am. I didn't sleep very well. Guess it's time to invest in a new mattress after all. Since when did mine have springs poking out. My eyes finally take in the room. This doesn't look like my bedroom. This room is too dark, and you can feel the dampness in the air. It smells musty, like a wet dog. That's when it all comes crashing back.

I must have banged my head because it took way longer than I thought for my mind to start working properly again. I feel the weight on my wrists, my skin prickles and my breath hitches. Now's not the time, Catalina. Rein it in bitch, and you gotta figure some shit out. With a couple of deep breaths, I slowly move my hands. The chains rattle, making a lump form in my throat. I turn to look. Handcuffs attached to a chain are locked on each wrist. I follow the chain to find it latched around a steel headboard. I shift my feet apart. Thank God. I can use them as a weapon.

Beads of sweat form along my hairline, and I become dizzy with every inch I move my hands; I hate this. I lay back down to try to calm down. I'm focusing on my breathing when the door flies open. I shift into a seating position with my back against the headboard. I take in my captor. He's still wearing that stupid neon mask, with a black hoodie to hide his hair and other features. He stands in the doorway, commanding control. He can suck my big toe if he expects me to bow at his feet.

"Aren't you going to ask why you're here, pretty girl?" His croaky voice echoes in the small room.

"Why? If you're expecting a ransom, I'd give up now."

He walks further into my humble adobe. "Catalina, you are an important piece to this story."

Goosebumps work all over my body. What goddamn story? Who the hell is this creep? Come closer so I can kick that stupid mask off your face, you prick. He must read my thoughts because he heads back to the door.

"I'll be back later. Don't go anywhere." He walks out of the room, slamming the door closed.

"Like I could if I wanted." I mock him.

I sink back into the bed, not sure what I'm supposed to do. My hands are literally tied behind my back. I don't even know where I am, and I'm still trying to figure out what he wants from me. I have nothing, and no one will pay to get me back, so he must be fuckin' desperate. Honestly, who pays ransoms these days? My mother wouldn't. She would laugh in his face, turn around and walk away. She'll probably yell at me, telling me I had it coming from being a whore. If she only knew. Fuck. Now I'm thinking of them. I was hoping I could go without memories of them. I can't go down that rabbit hole right now. From my observations, I noticed Cole's stunning blue eyes and defined jawline, the brown tousled hair and full lips of Nyx, and the captivating green eyes and tattooed skin of Dorian. It's genuinely wonderful to appreciate the unique features that make each person special.

Come to think of it, and I haven't seen Nyx or Dorian fully naked. I've seen the lower half, and I have no complaints. Ten out of ten would do it again. But I need to see the entire package.

Will I get that chance again? Cole kicked me out. Does that mean he's finished with me? Ugh. Now I'm getting pissed off again. I slowly work the cuffs so they sit comfortably. My skin still crawls, but at least I can control my breathing. I try to distract myself; I look up at the ceiling or lack thereof. It consists of rafters and wires. I try to follow them but lose them halfway when it gets too dark to see. Wouldn't it be amazing if humans had built-in night vision like cats? The things I would see and probably want to unsee.

Dear God, I'm going mad already. It hasn't even been that long. I furrow my brows. Or has it? I don't even know how long I was passed out for; he did hit me pretty good. Maybe this is a dream.

"You dummy, you can't smell in your dreams." Why am I so mean to myself?

I couldn't tell how long I sat here, waiting for dickface to come back. My stomach lets out a painful rumble, so guaranteed I've been here for at least a day. I close my eyes, thinking of anything besides being in this shitty basement.

A hand runs along my jaw. I'm in that weird phase of sleep where I'm somewhat aware of my surroundings, but it could be a dream. I'm pretty sure Dorian is touching me, but that can't be. I snap my eyes open, coming face to face with dickface. I pull away and growl.

"Don't fucking touch me."

He lets out a monotone laugh. "Now, pretty girl. Don't be like that. I came by with some food." He leans over, grabbing something off the floor. When he sits back up, he's holding a sandwich and a bottle of water.

I arch my black eyebrow at him. "How do I know you didn't poison it?" I question him.

I can hear him take a deep breath yes. Remove the mask and take a bite. Show me it's not poisoned, mother trucker. Then I can see you.

"Guess you'll have to believe me." He drops the water and puts the sandwich on my lap. "Better eat that before the mice come out." Standing, he heads back for the door.

"I still don't know what you want with me. If you're not gonna–"

"Abuse you? Pummel my fist into that face of yours? Or string you up from the ceiling naked and leave you hanging until someone hopefully finds you?" His voice turns malice like. Sending chills down my spine. "As I said, you're a piece of the story, and it's just the beginning."

The slam of the door rattles my bones. If I was hungry, I'm not anymore. I need to get the fuck out of this place. I'm not sticking around any longer than I have to, especially if that's the way he thinks. The only thing stopping me is these handcuffs and the headboard.

I turn around so I'm facing the headboard. I'm a little compromised in this position. My arms are crisscrossed, but at least I can see what I'm doing. I grab the bar between my hands, and with a tight grip, I spin it to the left. I keep trying until it loosens. The nice thing about old things is that they fall apart rather quickly. I take hold of the chain with both hands, and after a big inhale, I pull hard on the bar. The metal makes a loud clanging noise that echoes in my ears. I pause to listen for any approaching footsteps, but when I hear nothing, I give it another go. This time, I push harder and prop my feet against the wall for better balance.

Nothing. I need to bend the bar some so it can pop out of the holes.

"Work. With. Me." I grit my teeth as I pull the chain. My spirit is slowly fading when this plan of mine goes into the gutter. I try one more time because let's be honest. I'm losing steam, and I tossed that sandwich on the floor. Poisonous or not, I would've eaten it... eventually.

With my teeth clenched, I pull, tug, and yank.

My entire body flies backwards, my back landing on a spring that's poking out of the mattress.

"Ow." I rub my back. Wait. I can rub my back.

I gather up the chain, slipping off the bed. I get a cold chill from the cement floor on my socked feet. That bastard took my combat boots and my coat. I couldn't even tell you if it was day or night out. When my hand touches the doorknob, I get a little nervous. I'm five-two. I can't fight for shit. What am I going to do if I run into someone up there? There could be more than dickface up there.

I drag the door open, going in blind. I peer around the doorjamb. It opens to a large, empty room. I creep along the walk, trying not to shake the chains. It's so dark down here I can't see a fuckin' thing. Including...

"Fuuuuck." I limp around in a circle, trying to calm down. But it's safe to say my pinkie toe is done. I felt that one in my stomach. I breathe easy when I take in the stupid thing I stubbed my toe on. The staircase is right in front of me. The first step creaks a little, and I look up towards the door, holding my breath. Each step is slow, my heart trying to beat out of my chest. The last step, I place my ear against the door, listening for any sound. My trembling hand reaches for the knob, slowly turning it. I push it open.

I'm greeted with silence. It's dim up here. The only light coming in is from the streetlight shining through the front window. Looking around, I take in the sight of the run-down house. The living room is sad and grim, opening up to the kitchen that may have held incredible house parties at one time. Then again, the way it looks now, it hasn't seen anyone decent in years. I'm guessing slums have moved in, turning it into a drug house. It's good to know I'm still in Eastwood. Southside from the looks of this house. The floor is cluttered with garbage and broken bottles. To be honest, I'm sure there are needles and other drug paraphernalia that I'm unable to see. The living room appears to be empty, and nothing is in my way of that front door. *William Wallace* called. He wants his freedom back. I'm not one to stop that.

With one final look around, I step over a broken bottle, only to step into something wet. I'm not going to look or freak out; I'm glad to be wearing socks. The chains rattle together when I sway, a little fatigue setting in. After I find a way out of these stupid things, I'm getting a thick-ass burger. I finish the distance without any other incident. I don't even care if someone is on the other side of this door. I swing it open so fast the cold air leaves me breathless. The cold air nips at my skin as I step out into the night. As I suspected, I'm in Southside. This will be tricky: a woman running around with handcuffs on. That just screams easy prey.

I take off down the broken stairs. On a whim, I take a right down the street. I'll eventually figure out where I am and have to get off the main road. That's my goal. I keep running until I reach the first alley, darting down just in time as a car comes down the road. I place my hand over my heart, and it's beating like rapid-fire. I throw myself into a sprint, my feet screaming at me with every step I take.

The second I cross over the invisible line dividing the town, I slow my pace. Every muscle in my body is cramped with fatigue, and I'm so dizzy and tired.

Trudging along, I go to the only place I can think of.

3

COLE

I'm on pins and needles, waiting for Henry to get to the warehouse. We had time to return the van and grab our bikes. He'll never be the wiser on our little stunt. Or at least, I hope. When I joined the gang, Henry wasn't this crazy. He didn't care what people did around town and only cared about others producing drugs. He was the go-to for drugs and no one else. I think that's where it all went wrong. The power went to his head.

Growing up in this town, you only had two options if you weren't leaving it: Soul Stealers or Southside. Well, considering I came from Southside, I wasn't staying there. I knew what would happen if I did. I would've ended up either dead or in prison. So, I do owe Henry, but only for the last couple of months. Fuck that dick. I'm so over this.

I want out. I'm sure the guys want out as well. Our views have changed recently.

"He's here. He just walked in," Nyx whispered under his breath. He's standing in the torture room's doorway.

I dip my chin. "Let's get this over with, and then we can search for Cat." We both leave, walking into the common area where Dorian awaits us.

Henry takes notice of us, smiling so big it causes wrinkles to appear around his eyes. "Great work, boys. I knew I could count on you. It's a shame I couldn't have watched it. You all know how to work some magic, that's for sure."

I'm not sure how to take that. Is it a compliment, or are we sick bastards?

"Um, thanks, I guess."

"We need to discuss Conrad. I would like for him to join and become an enforcer."

All of our heads snap at him.

"How many do you need? Three isn't enough?" Dorian raises his voice. Nyx places his hand on his bicep to calm him.

Henry raises his hands in surrender. "It's not like that. You're all still in school. Sometimes I need shit done during the day–"

I cut him off to remind him. "It was your stupid idea for everyone to go to school."

"Yes, so you would owe me when you graduate. You don't think I would pay for your schooling for free, did you?" He shoots me a grin. "By going to school, you signed up to be my little bitch until your debt is paid off."

I should've known better. There is no getting out of this gang. It might not be blood in, blood out. We did have an initiation, and if you owed Henry a debt, you bet your ass you would have to pay it. If not, he sent the enforcers after you. We collected so many debts for him that it's unreal. I think he wants this gang to be more prominent, but his members refuse. Having Conrad join up is a problem. Nothing about this guy screams decent human being. It's not like I have a say in it. We just need to find a way to bring Henry down.

"No, Henry, I know better." My lips curl around the words. "If you don't mind, we had a late night and are tired."

"You have balls, kid. You should show me some respect before I beat it into you." I watch as his nostrils flare. At least I can still get him riled up.

I just turn and walk away. I'm fuckin' done. I push the doors open, getting blinded by the sun. It's hard to believe we worked throughout the night and early morning. It doesn't seem like it, but I guess when you're trying to disguise dead bodies to look like fresh dead bodies, it takes a lot out of you. My mind quickly wonders to Wednesday, wherever she is. I hope like hell she's safe.

"Let's get some rest, and we'll head out tonight to look for Cat. My gut is telling me she's still in town somewhere." I look at the guys as I climb on my Street Bob.

Nyx grips his handlebars until his knuckles turn white. He's staring off into the distance. I can tell he's taking it the hardest. He's used to seeing her almost every day in class, and his eyes find mine blinking slowly. He nods and fires up his bike. Dorian's face rumpled with sadness, with eyebrows perched low. I know this is hitting him hard, too. But we're all stubborn fucks and won't talk about it.

Once she's back, I'll have a lot of begging to do, and I'll give her anything she wants if I have to. As much as this kills me to think if she wants nothing to do with me, I'll walk away. I'm the one that keeps pushing her away all the time.

By the time we get home, we're all exhausted.

"Man, I'm so tired I can't even think straight." Dorian rubs his face roughly before getting off his bike.

"I hear ya, D. I'm about to drop dead," Nyx said with a yawn.

I open the front door for us. I always love coming home. We all purchased this house together. You could say it was love at first sight. Something about it called to us. I'm not sure about the darkness or how unwanted it was, sorta like all of us.

I wave to them as I climb the stairs leading to my room. It's not the same entering here after having her in here. It smells faintly like her if I inhale deep enough. I pull off my shirt and kick my boots off simultaneously, stumbling around. Fuck it. The pants can stay on. I fall face-first onto the bed.

I wake wrapped up in my blankets. My mind is still foggy, and I'm trying to figure out what day it is. When it finally clicks that, it's still the same day. Only much later, the sky is already growing dark. My stomach lets out a low groan. I guess it's been a while since I've eaten. I would love to lay in bed for a little longer, but Catalina is more important. We need a game plan. With no clues, we're in the dark about where to begin. It'll be like looking for a needle in a haystack. When I get downstairs, Dorian is already cooking.

"You know, you make the perfect kitchen bitch." I slap him on the back on my way to the table.

"Fuck off. If I didn't cook, you would starve."

"Well, you are a good cook, D. So." Nyx grins and hitches his shoulder at him. "What are you cooking, anyway?"

Dorian lets out a mumble. "Homemade macaroni and cheese."

My stomach releases another rumble. "How much longer? I'm not gonna last that long."

"Jesus, don't be rushin' me, or I'll make you two cook." He turns his back to us and goes back to cooking. Either way, he'll finish supper. This is how Dorian deals with stress when he can't think. He needs to cook. Having Cat gone is eating at him, and knowing we can't help kills me.

We hardly eat, but we come up with a plan to search the cemetery once more. We're thinking that maybe her captor accidentally dropped something of hers, or we can at least try to figure out which way they went. Not many people have been up to the cemetery between them and us. So, our chances are good.

We're all quiet as we get ready. Dressed in black, we look like we're about to get into trouble. The cops wouldn't even think about giving us any grief tonight. You couldn't tell we belonged to the gang, and we figured to keep it all under the radar. I jerk the front door open and pause.

"Hello, boys, did you miss me?" she huffed, her lips pulled into a grimace.

Catalina, the sight of her has my knees buckling. She's leaning against the house, alive. I'm looking her over for any injuries. She's shaking, only dressed in a t-shirt, leggings, and socks. Her wrists are locked in handcuffs. I don't know how she isn't breaking down right about now.

"Half pint," Dorian whispered from behind me.

Nyx rushes out, wrapping her in his arms and getting her in the house. That brings the fire under my ass working. He sits her on the couch, his fingertips travelling down her arm for her hand.

"Baby, we'll get these off you right away." He turns to me. "Bolt cutters?"

"Hold tight, Wednesday."

When I return with the bolt cutters, she's wrapped in a blanket, drinking a glass of water. When her violet eyes met mine, they were soft as a whisper. I lose myself more and more in the depths of her. I approach her, and her eyes shift to the bolt cutters.

"Don't worry. It'll be over quickly."

She takes a deep breath. "Okay. Cause I'm starving."

"It also means we need to talk."

"Yeah, whatever. Hurry, Cole." She holds her hands out for me.

Fuckin' little shit. I make quick work getting these off her. The metal hits the floor, and her entire body relaxes. Her wrists have bloody red marks from being rubbed raw against the cuffs. I gently take them in mine, running my thumbs over them.

"How do you feel?" I look up at her, and she's staring at her wrist grimly.

"I don't understand why all this is happening to me." Her voice is wavering.

Nyx moves next to her, placing a hand on her thigh, while Dorian stands behind the couch, placing a hand on her shoulder. We're all giving her a little bit of our strength.

"I'll grab you something to eat, and then you can fill us in." I stand, placing a kiss on her forehead. It takes everything inside of me to leave her side. I eventually go and head to the kitchen. I pull open the fridge, trying to think what to get her. This should've been Dorian in here, not me. What was I thinking? I delve into the fridge to find some leftovers. I can't fuck that up. Placing her food on a tray, I carefully walk back into the living room. Small chatter greets my ears before I take in the scene in front of me. Nyx is lying on the couch with Cat between his legs, and Dorian looks at her feet. I walk around, placing her food down on the coffee table.

"What's wrong with your feet?" I grab a bowl of reheated macaroni and cheese for her.

"That masked prick took my boots. I'm glad I had socks on, but running sorta did my feet in." She wiggles her toes, then groans.

"Hold still, half-pint. You still have some slivers in there."

"Sorry," she mutters around a mouth full of food. "This is good. Who cooked?"

We all laugh. "The only decent cook in the house is Dorian. Don't get me wrong, I can cook, but it's question-able." Nyx discloses his dirty little secret.

She looks at me. "Same."

"To be honest, I haven't eaten in a while, so it could taste like dog shit, and I would still eat it." She shovels another mouthful of food into her mouth, not caring about manners.

I hate to kill her good mood, but I think it's time for her to tell us what the hell happened. If I'd ever taken someone, they usually didn't look like themselves, so why the hell did this person take her? I need answers, and I'm trying to control myself from getting them from her. The longer we wait, the more time her captor has to escape.

"Wednesday, I need to know. How did you get away?"

She places her fork into her bowl and passes it to me. "I was hoping to get a shower before we talked about it."

"Sorry, baby, but I think we all want to know—need to know." Nyx rubs her shoulders, comforting and reassur-ing her.

She takes one big deep inhale.

4

CATALINA

"Wednesday, I need to know. How did you get away?" Cole looks at me with sorrow.

I place my fork into my bowl and pass it to Cole. "I was hoping to get a shower before we talked about it."

"Sorry, baby, but I think we all want to know—need to know." Nyx rubs my shoulders. I can feel his warm hands working my muscles and calming me down.

I close my eyes, taking a deep, cleansing breath and trying to figure out where to start. My mind is one big jumble of a mess.

"Just start from where you want to. We won't rush you." Dorian's husky voice sent a thrill through my body. Probably not the time to be thinking these thoughts, Cat.

"Okay, I was working in the cemetery, taking my time. I had two bodies, and there was no rush for them. I guess that's my fault. If I didn't dog fuck I would've been finished sooner. Maybe then he wouldn't have gotten to me." Three sets of hands squeeze my body. I look up at the ceiling when my eyes sting. I will not fuckin' cry. "I tried. I even grabbed my bear spray but fell into the grave during my run." Cole's finger brushes my hair away from my face.

"This explains the scratch, then."

"It doesn't hurt now. Glad it's not deep, but I'm getting used to head injuries." I let out a nervous laugh. We all know what happened the first night with them. I catch them up with my escape, trying to fill in the blanks and all their questions.

"The only thing I'm trying to figure out is why he didn't have any demands or try to call anyone. Why kidnap you?" Dorian questioned.

"He says it's all part of the plan." Which I'm still trying to figure out what that means. He doesn't seem familiar to me. That's what's driving me up the wall. "Now he'll be waiting for me everywhere I go. He should've figured out by now that I'm gone."

"I think we should head back to that house and scope it out, and if he does return, I say we give him a Soul Stealers welcome," Cole growls, looking at me like he would burn the world down before letting me go again. It's too bad he couldn't look at me like that before this happened.

"Do you think that's a good idea?"

"No offence, baby, this is the best idea. If we catch him, then this nightmare will be over right away. You'll be safe."

I place my hand over Nyx's heart. "I just don't want any of you to get hurt because of me. I'm not worth it." All three of them growl at me.

"Listen to me right now, darling. You are the most important person to me—us. We've met no one as unique as you. That's what I love about you. Trust me, if we wanted someone like everyone else, we would've picked a normal girl. But we want you because you are worth it. You are worth it because you never fake it with us. You show us your true self and are never afraid of who you are. So don't you dare say you are not worth it." Dorian crawls up my body and drops a kiss on the tip of my nose. "Do you understand me?"

"Yes," I say, blinking back tears. I've never had anyone that cared this much for me, let alone three people at once. It's too much for me to process. I go to stand, but Nyx stops me.

"Where are you going?"

"I just need some time to process all this and a shower. I'm sorry. I just never had anyone on my team before. I don't know what to do."

"You lean on us. You trust us."

I look into Coles' deep blue eyes. "I trusted you, and you fuckin' stepped all over my heart. How can I ever trust you again?"

He dips his head. "You don't. I don't expect you to—"

"Good, 'cause it's not gonna happen. I forgave you once already easily, and I won't do it again, Cole."

I get up and start for the stairs. I have no idea where I'm headed. I've only been to two rooms in this house, so I can't go wrong searching. My feet ache with every step I take. I take the familiar hallway instead of going to the nasty all-white bedroom. I pass it, walking into the room next to it. Pushing open the door, I take in the spice and citrus smell. From the scent alone, I can tell this is Nyx's room. I inhale deeply and relax the further I walk into his room. I take in how clean his room is. His room is beautiful, and the bay window is the perfect spot for reading or painting. I push away the curtains, looking out to the empty, dark street.

"What are you looking at, baby?"

The sound of Nyx's voice causes me to jump. "Sorry." Turning around to face him. "I wasn't snooping, I swear."

He walks closer to me, grabbing my hand. "I know, don't worry. Want me to start a bath for you?"

I lean into his chest. "That would be amazing." He rubs my back before heading into his insight. The sound of running water fills the bedroom. I stand at the door, watching him add Epsom salts to the water, swirling it around in the water. He must sense my presence because he turns and smiles at me.

"Get undressed. The water is perfect." He doesn't move and makes himself comfortable on the tub's edge.

I walk further into the bathroom. I pull my t-shirt over my head, dropping it on the tiled floor. I watch as his green eyes become darker. I slide my hands down my stomach, getting a groan out of him. I turn around and bend over as I push my leggings down, showing off my ass.

"Fuck, baby. What I wouldn't do right now to be fucking that ass."

My pussy aches when he talks like that. I've never had more than a finger, so taking a cock makes me nervous. Except I trust him, I believe he would take good care of me and wouldn't hurt me. I slowly stand, running my hand up my legs. I've given no one a strip tease before, but the sounds he's making, I take it I'm doing a good job.

"You're killing me, baby." He repositions himself, and my stomach flutters at the sight.

I unclasp my bra, letting it fall to the floor. My nipples tighten either from the cooler air or from the way Nyx is currently examining me. I run my fingers along the seam of my thong, dipping lower each time. I'm about to slip them off when I stop.

"All right, big guy, out you get."

His eyes widen to the size of dinner plates. "Are you fuckin' kidding me? You get me this turned on to stop?" He stands, marching his way toward me. He's like a lion stalking his prey. I hold my position, never taking my eyes off him. "You know what I want, baby?" he asks when he gets right in front of me.

"No," I whispered.

He grips my chin, moving my face to the side. Running his nose alongside my neck, he nips his way toward my ear. I let out a small moan. When his hands slip into my hair, he releases my ponytail, running his fingers through it.

"That feels nice. Can I be honest with you for a minute?"

He keeps massaging my scalp. "Baby, I always want you to be honest with me."

I swallow to clear the knot that has grown. "I didn't think I would get out of that basement, let alone unharmed. My only thought was getting back here to you three, and I'm not sure what I would do if something happened."

He pulls me into his chest, rubbing his warm hands against my naked skin. "Shh, we wouldn't let that happen, baby. We would've gone to the world's end to find you."

The sob that left me was painful, shaking my body terribly. I honestly thought my captor would've hung me from the fuckin' rafters, leaving me there until they found my body. Now he's out there still, waiting for me. I should get Cole to scope out the house I left, and it's probably the only chance we have at finding who did this to me.

"Can you have a bath with me? I don't want to be alone at the moment." Nyx wipes my tears away when I look up at him.

"I would do anything you ask of me, baby." He steps back, pulling his shirt over his head. My eyes work over his sculpted body; he may be the smallest out of the three of them, but he's still very much built. Then, I catch the piercings in each of his nipples. I raise my eyebrow at him.

He chuckles at me. "Don't ask. It was a dare. Don't dare me to do something. I'm gonna fuckin' do it."

"Is that a fact?"

"Get in the tub before I dare you to do something you won't be able to back out of."

I step into the hot water, lowering myself. I let out a moan when my entire body immerses in the water. Nyx steps up to the tub, fully naked. I can't help but lick my lips, moving forward, he climbs in behind me. The water sloshes over the side as his long legs wrap around mine. He runs his hands up my arms to my hair again, moving it out of my face. He leans down, kissing my cheek.

"I don't want you to ever worry about anything, do you understand? The three of us will take care of you even if Cole sometimes can't get his head out of his ass. He just has a hard time with the whole filter thing."

I shot him a scoff. "No shit. But I'm getting tired of being his punching bag. If he can't figure his shit out, I will not take it much longer. He's lucky that he gets a second chance. Usually, I don't believe in them; if I recall, this is his third now."

"Lucky number three?"

"He better not blow it." I lean further back into his chest, feeling his heartbeat against my back. Closing my eyes, I've never felt more relaxed or at home.

"He won't. I trust him this time, baby." He tips my head back, getting my hair wet. "Let's not worry about him right now; you need to relax and rest. We can worry about everything tomorrow."

I have a hard time concentrating. Nothing feels better than someone else washing your hair. I stifle a moan when he continues to massage deeper. When his hands work their way lower on my body, all thoughts leave the second his fingers pinch my nipples. I can feel him growing thicker behind me; I can't help but wiggle my ass.

"Careful, I might do something to that ass."

Oh, sweet Jesus. Yes, I want that more than anything. "Please, I want you so bad."

"Get out and get on that bed." His voice turns husky. Usually, he is never one for being demanding. I shiver hard when I step out of the tub. I'm not sure from the air or his words; I can't wait for what's coming. I lay on the bed waiting for him. He's taking his time getting his ass in here, and I'm getting more worked up the longer he takes. The bedroom door opens, and Dorian walks in.

"This looks entertaining. Mind if I join?" He walks over to the bed, kneeling just above me. His gaze sets my body on fire. I lick my lips when he runs his hands alongside my ribs. My stomach flutters when I feel Nyx's hands on my legs. Holy shit, this is happening.

"Think you can handle both of us? Together?" Nyx asked between kisses.

I have to close my eyes to answer him, or I won't be able to concentrate. "What do you mean, together?" I've already taken them together, so why would he ask?

They both chuckle. "Both holes, baby."

"Holy shit."

"Spread your legs wide for me; your body is ours tonight, baby."

I do what he says, growing wetter by the second. Dorian pinches my left nipple, making me arch my back and dig my heels into the bed. Nyx takes that moment to drag his finger into my wet needy pussy. I let out a strangled moan, waiting for him to touch me where I was most desperate, but he never did.

"Nyx, please." I whimper. I try to move my hips to reach his hand, but he tightens his hold around my thigh. Dorian takes pity on me by drawing a nipple into his mouth. Sucking hard, then flicking my nipple with his tongue. He bites my nipple, pulling it upwards before releasing it. I whimper before he heads to the other one.

I hear a bottle open, then cold wetness on my ass. I let out a gasp.

"Don't worry. I have to prep you first. Relax." I try, but I'm nervous. Dorian's hand slips between us, down my stomach. He finds my clit and starts rubbing it gently. I felt pressure in my ass, causing me to tighten up again.

"It's a plug. Focus on what Dorian is doing. Feel his fingers run along that pretty little pussy of yours." Dorian moves his lips along my collar, sucking hard in random places. The sensation of that and the pressure from both working me down below send me over the top. I plunge into my orgasm without warning, screaming my release, clenching my fingers into the blanket. When I finally relax, both guys are waiting for me.

Nyx crawls up on the bed beside me, cupping my face. "So beautiful. We'll take things slow, okay?"

I can only nod; my body is still tingling, and if I move my hips, I can feel the plug hit at a certain angle. "I'm ready for both of you, but Dorian is still overdressed." I look over at my blonde God to see him still fully dressed. He gives me a light chuckle before grabbing the hem of his shirt and slowly sliding it up his body. His sculpted abs display a collection of tattoos on his torso. Once his shirt hits the ground, I'm already moving toward him. My fingers dig into the waist of his jeans, pulling him closer. I kiss his stomach, causing him to groan.

"Fuck..." His hands dig into my hair, pulling my head back. He leans down, kissing me deeply. Releasing me slowly, he steps back, unbuttoning his jeans. They slid off his hips, leaving him commando, his thick thighs flexing when he stepped out of his jeans. Nyx takes this moment to wrap his arms around my waist, pulling me back to the bed.

"Up on your knees."

I struggle to shift with the pressure building again. With every squeeze, the plug moves in and out of me. Nyx's hand runs along my ass cheek before he lands a loud smack. My pussy clenches, needing attention.

"I need more." I push my ass back until I touch Nyx. His fingers run along my slit towards my ass. I whimper when he lightly tugs at the plug. Feeling a light tug, I completely relax, allowing him to effortlessly remove it.

"Such a good girl. Think you can handle more?"

"Yes, I want both of you at the same time."

Nyx grabs the lube bottle and squirts it over himself and me. His hand lands on my hips, pulling me closer to him. He runs the tip over my tight entrance and pushes forward slowly. I hiss when I feel slight pressure.

"You okay?"

"Ya, I'm good. Keep going." He pushes forward more, getting past the tight muscle. I take a deep inhale the further he pushes in. He pauses, giving me time to catch my breath. I feel so full, and he's not even in all the way. Dorian kneels next to me. I take that moment to clasp my hand around his shaft. Nyx pushes the rest of the way inside the force, causing me to grip Dorian harder.

"Shit, darling." He hissed.

Nyx takes it slowly so as not to overwhelm me, and I press back into him when he comes forward, and I need more. When he pulls out, I whimper at the loss.

"Don't worry. Dorian, lay down, baby, get on top." We do as he says. I crawl over Dorian rubbing my pussy on his cock. His hands come up to my breasts, squeezing them. I reach between us, slipping him inside. With slow, controlled movements, I rock my hips forwards, worshiping his thick cock.

I never thought I would be back here, especially with both men. Getting kidnapped brings a new perspective to your life, that's for sure. If I never escaped, what then? Nyx lays a hand on my back, pushing my chest to Dorians, getting me to leave my thoughts behind. He rubs my lower back while Dorian drives upwards, coaxing my orgasm closer.

Smack. "You don't come yet, baby girl. You wait until I'm inside of you first."

My pussy instantly clamps around Dorian. Nyx lines up behind us, making Dorian come to a stop. My toes curl, and I throw my head back when Nyx enters me fully. My breaths are coming out rapidly when he moves forward, and Dorian moves backwards. They work in tandem, bringing me to ecstasy. I tighten around each of them, getting growls and grunts in return. It's like feeling drunk.

My world is spinning, but I'm being held and secured. I know they won't let anything happen to me. I fall deeper into Dorian's chest, kissing his shoulder.

Dorian drives one final push before going still as he finishes with a deep moan, gripping my waist as he finishes deep inside of me. He kisses along my collar before touching my forehead. Nyx smacks me again before running his hand around my throat, pulling me to his chest as he pounds into me hard. I let out a stifled scream as I took him.

"I own this ass... *thrust...* do you understand... *thrust.*"

I gasp when he lets go of me, and he goes, still shooting his cum in my ass. He slowly pulls out, letting Dorian do the same thing. Nyx rolls over onto his back, letting me curl into his side. Dorian turns over, trailing kisses down my neck. I kiss Nyx on the chest as my eyes grow heavy.

"Good night, baby." He leaves a kiss on my forehead.

"Good night, darling." Dorian leaves a kiss on the back of my head.

The last thing I remember before falling asleep is the sound of Cole's door closing.

5

CATALINA

The next morning, I woke up alone, not how I wanted to, especially after how yesterday went. Guess I can't have my cake and all that shit. Or, however, that saying goes. As much as I don't want to leave this warm bed, I have to. I need to get my ass back to school and start figuring out who the hell is after me. I give my achy body a good stretch, feeling my joints crack and release.

Reluctantly, I climb out, searching for my clothes. I'll also need to head home to get clean clothes. I ditch mine to search through Nyx's dresser, finding a t-shirt and a pair of sweatpants. Pulling his t-shirt up to my nose, I take a deep inhale. It smells of spice and citrus, just like him.

I step into the kitchen to see Cole is staring out the window, drinking his coffee. He is not the person I want to be seeing first thing, especially after his rude dismissal a week ago. Am I still salty about it? Fuck yeah. I may have let him have a free pass last night since everyone wanted information, but that dickwad can kiss the bottom of my feet now. He doesn't say a thing while I walk to the coffee pot and still doesn't say a thing as I sit down at the table. I do my business drinking my bean juice, waiting for Dorian and Nyx to reappear wherever they are.

"You don't owe me anything." Cole's husky voice cuts the silence of the room. "What I did to you was un-called for. I have a hard time dealing with my emotions sometimes. The thought of this being our fault doesn't sit right, and I didn't want you in the middle of it. I thought pushing you away would keep you safe." He finally turns with his head bowed, his shoulders slumped. He ran his hand through his already tousled hair. "I know I can't ask for your forgiveness, so when you're ready, can we try again?"

I focus on my coffee like it's the most crucial thing in the room, his words running through my head. He might have thought at the time it was the best thing, but he could've gone around it differently.

I drum my fingers on the table, thinking about how to explain things to him. "Cole, I—you left me wounded. Giving another chance will be your last one when I'm ready. For now, you're just a friend, nothing more."

He closes his eyes and nods. "I can agree to that. Thank you, Weds—Catalina."

"Baby, nice to see you up and wearing my clothes." Nyx leans over me, cupping my chin. Staring into my eyes, he kisses me gently on the lips. Before it can grow deeper, he pulls away. Dorian comes up next, placing a kiss on my forehead.

"Morning, half pint."

I notice Cole slipping away to the stairs. I guess he doesn't want to hang around if he's only a friend now. "Where were you two?"

"Hittin' up the gym needed to work off some pent-up energy." Nyx goes about mixing a protein shake for himself and Dorian. "We have to figure some things out. We all agreed you're not returning to your apartment until this creep is caught. We can move you into the guest room." I go to interrupt, but he holds his hand up. "I'm not going to take no, so you'll do as we say."

"Is that so? I didn't realize that you are the boss of me suddenly." I cross my arms over my chest, staring up at him.

"Don't be like that half pint; it's for your own good, and you know it. So, we'll head to your place if you're ready."

I guess that's the end of that discussion.

Having all three guys in my tiny ass place is overwhelming, to say the least. I leave them to do their own thing. I'm not one to entertain. *Apparently,* I have a bag to pack. For how long, I'm not even sure cause if they think I'm letting them rule my life, they are sadly mistaken. I throw a bunch of random clothes in my bag, then wander into the bathroom. I'm gathering the essentials when raised voices come from the living room.

The scene before me should only be seen on the football field. I'm surprised Cole and Dorian haven't fallen through my floor yet.

"What the fuck is going on!" I yell at all three of these dicks.

Their motions halt immediately. It would be comical in different circumstances. Dorian has Cole pinned to the ground—Dorian's biceps flex, trying to hold a struggling Cole still.

"Stop fighting me already," Dorian growled.

"You're not the boss of me, asshat. So, get the fuck off of me before I beat the shit out of you."

Dorian sinks lower to Cole's face. "I'd like to see you try."

"All right, that's enough, you two. Will someone tell me what the hell is happening? I leave for five minutes, and World War Three breaks out." I give them both a disapproving headshake. I've never seen them fight before, especially like this.

Dorian pushes off Cole's chest, not without glaring at him. Cole gets up, dusting imaginary dirt off his pants. He brushes past Dorian, knocking him back before storming down the hall to the bathroom. I turn back to Dorian, raising my eyebrow, waiting for him to explain all of this shit.

With a huff, he finally spilled his guts. "He said a few things, and I flew off the handle, okay?"

"No, it's not okay. What kind of explanation is that?" I raise my hands in the air.

He goes to the couch, slumping in a heap, resting his forearms on his knees. "Cole was saying some shit about how he should've done more, and he was blaming himself. He was ready to storm out of here and do God knows what. That's when we started fighting, and I had to take him down forcefully."

"I've never seen anything like this before, baby. Cole has never acted out to this extent before." Arms wrap around my waist, and Nyx places gentle kisses against my neck. "I think he blames himself for everything that has happened to you."

I lean back in his embrace. "Well, he shouldn't. It wasn't just his fault if you think about it. You guys ignored me, too. Somehow, I have forgiven you a lot easier." I mumble the last part, primarily to myself.

"I won't listen to that anymore. I was to blame, you understand." Cole's booming voice cuts in from across the apartment. "I shouldn't have done what I did, end of fucking story. I'll forever be making it up to you, and there's no arguing. Grab your shit. We have to go." He marches to the door, leaving without another word.

Alrighty then, I guess that's that. Coles is back to himself after probably giving himself a manly pep talk in the bathroom surrounded by girl products. Pinching the bridge of my nose, I leave Nyx's warm arms and grab my bag.

"Come on, let's get this show on the road. Mr. Grump doesn't like to be kept waiting."

"Damn right, he doesn't." Dorian comes up alongside me, grabbing my bag from my hand. "Get used to it. And Cole has mood swings worse than a woman."

Trust me, I've noticed that, and we haven't even hung around that much. With one last look around, I leave my place, and I'll be so out of my element living with other people. I've been so used to doing things my way that I don't know what to do with others at home. The one thing I'll have a hard time giving up is the quietness—walking out of my apartment with my two men on either side, protecting me from preying eyes. I would have three, but Cole can't figure his shit out long enough. I noticed the growing number of blacked-out SUVs coming into town on the drive back to their place.

"That's for the mayor's meeting that's happening this week, and it's his turn to host it." There was an edge to Cole's voice that I couldn't place. I turned to face him in the rear-view mirror. His eyes darkened when they met mine. "We probably won't be around much this week. I need you to listen to what I tell you." Before I could tell him to fuck off, he turned his eyes back to the road. "Stay in the house when we aren't home, lock the fuckin door and don't answer it for no one. I'm serious, Catalina."

Pick your battles, Cat.

I have a feeling I won't be winning this one. By the time we pull into the driveway, I'm itching to get out of this car. I miss Johnny. The first chance I get, I'm getting her. I can't live without that car. Everything else, yes, but not my baby. I swear newer cars give me an itch—especially ones filled with tension. No one talked since Cole told me what

I would be doing. The only reassurance I had was Nyx caressing my thigh the entire ride. His hand drifted higher inch by inch, turning me on by the second. My body was hotter than hell, yet he wouldn't touch me where I needed him the most. I was beyond sexually frustrated when I walked into the house. I hear him chuckle from behind me.

"You think that's funny? You just wait and see what I can do to you, hot shot."

Arms are wrapped around me, pulling me into his muscled body. "You think so, baby girl."

I twist around, bringing my lips to his. "I know so." I palm his growing bulge, getting him nice and hard. He moans when I kiss him. I pull away before he can hold me closer and head for the kitchen.

"Get back here, you witch."

"No, siree bob. I told you I'd get you back. Go take care of that boner you're sporting." I shoo him away from over my shoulder.

"Un-fuckin-believable." I hear him mutter to himself on his way up the stairs.

Dorian is already prepping something to eat, which shouldn't surprise anyone by now. He's the momma bear of the family. We'd all starve if he didn't feed our asses.

"What ya cooking?" I pull out a stool from the island to snag front-row seating.

He sets his pot down. "I'm going to make some minestrone soup from scratch."

A man who can cook and gives incredible orgasms. What else can he do?

"Who taught you to cook like this?" I watch as he brings all his ingredients, outlining everything in order. He was quiet before he answered me.

"It was my grandmother who taught me everything to know about cooking. I spent almost all of my childhood at her house. When she passed, I kept cooking, so I always held a part of her close to me."

"I'm sorry, Dorian. She would be extremely proud of you."

He gives me a small smile. "I hope so, half pint."

I watch him cook and send a silent thank you to his grandmother for teaching him everything she knew. When we all pile into the kitchen for supper, I notice Cole is somewhat in a good mood. At least when I smiled at him, he returned it. If he wants this to get further than the friend stage, he better get over the mood swings.

"I'm letting all of you know right now. I'm headed back to class tomorrow. If I don't attend, my scholarship is toast."

Cole stiffens, and Dorian stops chewing, but Nyx just beams with pride. That's because he gets the pleasure of sitting with me in philosophy.

6

COLE

This friend thing is complete bullshit. It's been three days since she's been back, and I haven't had her to myself since. How the hell am I supposed to get back to where we were if I can't even have a minute of her time? Having the mayor's stupid meeting also doesn't help. Henry has elected all of us to patrol City Hall. To top it all off, Catalina decided to leave without us knowing to grab her fucking car. I've never been more pissed off than I was when she skipped through the door, all while she smiled, swinging her car keys on her finger. That was until I flew off the handle and landed myself back in the goddamn doghouse.

I need to figure something out, and there have to be some clues on what to do cause god knows I can't for the life of me figure out what I'm supposed to do to make her want me. Being away from her again today isn't helping me relax. That fuckin' creep can be around, and I knew we should've hit up his house the night she came home. I was too busy licking my wounds.

"I need a game plan, Cole. We can't be out here all night again. If nothing's happened, yet I don't think anything is going to happen."

That's another thing: Dorian keeps acting like King fuckin' Kong ever since Catalina moved in. I'm not sure why he thinks he's suddenly the boss, but I'm not liking it.

"Do you think I like leaving her home alone? If Henry suspects us of slacking, then what? He already brought Conrad in, which I'm surprised he isn't up our asses on this job to make sure we're doing everything correctly." I lean my forearms on my handlebars, looking towards the City Hall.

Nyx scoffs. "Don't even get me started on that twat. There's something off about him, and I can't figure it out."

"I feel the same way ever since he was introduced to us. He's never to meet Cat." Dorian adds.

We all nod in agreement. There are some things I don't mind keeping hidden.

I was ready to call it a night when I caught something out of the corner of my eye. A dude is scaling the fence to get into the building. I give a quiet whistle to get the guy's attention and gesture towards the figure. We slowly dismount from our bikes. Reaching for my desert eagle cocking it when we cross the road, by the time we reach the fence, our mysterious visitor is already across the lawn, making his way for the door. I give the guys commands to split up and deal with this guy however they see fit.

I head north, trying to round him up that way. When I notice another figure cutting through the west gate, I take off in that direction instead. Whoever these guys are, they aren't going to finish their task tonight. I've been itching to find a fight, and it looks like I finally found one. With quick, light footsteps, I take off. I stop at the edge of the rock garden, finding the biggest rock I can. I pitch it toward his head. He didn't even know what hit him. His body falls forward, kissing the ground. Rushing towards him, I kneel on his back, pressing my gun into his head.

"Who the fuck sent you?" I growl, finger twitching on the trigger.

He struggles to break free, causing me to press more of my body weight on him. "I'm not going to ask again fuck face. Tell me now."

"Why the fuck should I? We both know I'm a dead man either way."

I dig my gun further into his head. "At least you'll know where this will end for you. But I'm not one to wear brain matter." I haul the fucker up by the back of his shirt, pushing him toward the others. A loud whistle comes from my left, and I steer us in that direction, pushing my prisoner along the way.

"Watch where you're digging that thing," Dickhead growls at me. Like he has a place to tell me what to do. I push my gun harder into his back, making him trip over his feet.

"Hey Cole, we caught two more creeping before they snuck in. What should we do with them?" Nyx hollers from up ahead. When I get closer, I can finally see the two captive cunts on their knees with their arms behind their head. With one final push, mine goes down next to the others.

"I'll call Royce to ask him to bring the van. We'll bring them back to the torture room. Then get an answer that way."

I turn away, dialling Royce. He tells me it'll be at least twenty minutes when I explain everything to him. Fucking bullshit, but nothing I can do about it. Now we have twenty minutes of holding these asshats here without being noticed. Easier said than done.

Especially in this town.

Of course, my prisoner is the only one who has to cause us grief.

"You should just put us out of our misery. We ain't gonna say shit. Either you do it, or I'll find a way to end us."

"Will you just shut the fuck up already? You're giving me a migraine." Nyx smacks him on the back of the head.

The more I think about it, the brain matter would've been worth it. He keeps talking shit as I tune him out. I'll have my fun with him soon. I think I'll let him sit in the room overnight. We've been gone too long, and I won't be able to concentrate knowing that Cat is alone—*pop, pop.* The sound of gunfire has me ducking down low.

"What the hell is going on?" Dorian yelled.

"Fuck if I know, anyone hit?" I look around, gripping my gun—*pop, pop.*

"I'm good, you? Where the hell is that coming from?"

I finally take a look at the prisoners, and that's when I notice two are dead. Fuck. They must've had a team waiting somewhere that we didn't know about. Motherfuckers.

"Grab him and fucking run!" I yell. I took off toward where the shots were coming from. Hell's if I'm losing my last captive before I get answers. Rounding the corner of the hall, I see a blacked-out van pulling away. I aim my gun and fire off a couple of rounds, and I shoot out the back windows before they disappear into the dark. Cunts. I make my way back to the guys to find them by their bikes. Thankfully Royce has shown up and is shoving the last dickhead inside.

"They got away, a blacked-out cargo van. I got a few rounds in it but didn't catch any sight of who was driving." I slump next to my bike, feeling lightheaded unexpectedly.

"Cole." Dorian's hand is cupping my elbow, stabilizing my sinking knees. "Man, you got shot."

I let out a small laugh. "*No*, you don't fuckin' say, bud." I look over at my arm to see the blood leaking all the way to my hand. Moving it makes me wince. "At least it was an arm wound and nothing else."

"Can you ride? I'll call the doc to meet at the warehouse."

"I'm good. Let's go." I mount my bike, pissed that we won't be getting home early now.

The house is silent when we get home, and I wasn't expecting her to stay up for us. It's nearly three am. I'm tired, so I can only imagine how the other two feel. We're barely in the living room when the lamp is flicked on. There, sitting on the couch wrapped up in a blanket, is the beauty herself.

"What took you so long?" She surveys all three of us.

Dorian scratches the back of his neck. "We sorta had some problems. We should've called."

"God damn rights you should've called. What happened?"

I clear my throat. "We were ambushed, and I took a hit, no big deal. Head to bed Wednesday. You have class tomorrow." I head for the kitchen, ending this conversation. I'm not one to dwell on shit. I need a stiff drink. The doc shot my arm up with local anesthesia, but I can feel it coming out.

"Hold up, Cole. What the hell do you mean you took a hit?"

I let out a harsh sigh, rubbing my eyes. "What does it sound like? I got shot in the arm." I point to my bandaged arm.

Her eyes go wide. "Shit, Cole, are you okay?" She rushes towards me, grabbing my arm gently. "How did this happen? Do you need anything?" Her violet, concerned eyes meet mine.

"It's fine, don't fuss over me. The doc patched me up." I place my hand over hers, and feeling our connection again sends a jolt to my lower stomach. If only she were ready to move our friendship to the next level. "Get to bed Wednesday, please." I kiss her palm before turning away. The less temptation, the better. I walk past a waiting Dorian and Nyx. It looks like I'll be sleeping alone again tonight.

My bed was already calling my name by the time I reached the top of the stairs to my floor. I painfully peel my t-shirt off on my way to the bathroom. No matter how much I want to pass out, I need to wash this night off. The steam from the shower quickly fills the room. Rounding my back to the shower, I tip my head under the running water when fingers trace across my stomach. I snap my head towards the opening to see Catalina wearing only a smirk.

"If you're in here, you know what that means, don't you?"

She moves into the shower, brushing her tight nipples against my chest, arousing me more.

Her fingers slide further down my stomach, stopping at my pubic piercing. "I do, Cole. I could've lost you today if things had turned out worse. I can't do this anymore." She moves her hand lower, circling her hand around my shaft. I throw my head back with a moan. It's been a long while since she touched me. I almost forgot what she felt like. I grip the back of her hair, pulling her head back and making her groan, that sexy sound I love to hear. I lower my lips closer to her, tracing them with my tongue. She grips me tighter when I nip her lower lip. Pressing my lips to hers, I never want to be anywhere else.

"Fuck, I'm going to make you scream my name." I reach for the handheld shower head, switching the setting to pulse. "Hands on the wall, arch that back for me."

She lets out a small whimper when I run my hand along her back, getting her into position. "Good girl, it's gonna be fast tonight, but you'll still come for me, won't you?"

She nods. "Yes."

I kick her legs wider for me, her pussy on display. I run my finger between her lips and hips and kick back when I find her clit. Running the shower up her leg, she moans louder.

"Cole, stop teasing me."

I smirk. "Oh, little one, you would know if I was teasing." Her body stiffens with her oncoming climax when I pull away. She lets out a whine. I run the shower up higher, hitting her inner thigh close enough that she can feel the vibration on her pussy. I return my fingers, only this time I push them inside her.

"Oh, shit," she screams.

When she tightens again, I pull out.

"Okay, I get it." She trembles beneath me.

"That's me teasing you. Do you deserve to come?"

She nods. *Smack.* "Words, little one."

"Yes! I deserve to come."

I slam into her without warning, moving the shower head onto her clit. I have to grit my teeth with the hold she has on me already. I hold onto her hip as I unleash all my pent-up frustration into her. I move the shower head closer to her clit to bring her closer to her climax.

"Cole, please."

"I know. Come for me."

I pound harder, feeling her walls clamp around me. I work harder through the resistance. When her body shakes, I drop the showerhead and grab her. I pick her up, kissing her as we both find our release together. Once we find our breath again, I let her down. She looks dazed but does so with a smile on her face.

"Please don't fuck this up again, Cole."

"I won't, I swear." Shutting off the water, I find her a towel. Once we are both dried off, we finally head to bed.

Tomorrow will be one busy day, and I'm thankful I have her back cause I'm going to need her more than anything.

7

NYX

The smell coming from the torture room made me want to throw up Dorian's breakfast he cooked this morning. This motherfucker sitting in front of us decided to shit himself. Pulling my shirt over my nose, I walk further into the room, followed by Cole and Dorian.

"Jesus Christ, you are disgusting. If you think this will stop us from touching you, you're sadly mistaken. Maybe I'll rub your nose in it." Cole glares his deep blue eyes at the dickhole. He grabs the bolt cutters and walks over to the table filled with tools. I can see our friend shaking in his seat now.

"I still ain't talkin', so do what you have to. You saw what we do to our own."

Dorian moves closer, lowering his giant body to his level. "Wanna make a bet on it? You'll be squealing like a pig by the time Cole's finished with you. If he can't, then there's two more of us." He wiggles his eyebrows. "Name, or I'll give you one."

Dickhole spits on Dorian. Wrong move. I can see the change quickly. With one move, Dorian's fist lands on dickhole's jaw, snapping his face in the opposite direction. I wince when I hear the distinctive cracking of a broken jaw.

"Spit on me again. A broken jaw will be the least of your worries." He wrenches away, coming back to my side. "Fucking cunt," he mumbled.

Cole steps up, opening and closing the bolt cutters, taunting him with a mischievous grin. "Talk. Who hired you to attack the City Hall when all the mayors are present at the same time?"

Tight-lipped. Staring straight at the wall, I guess he doesn't take us seriously. I move in, grabbing his hand and straitening his fingers for Cole. I have to fight to get at least one finger straight. Cole opens the bolt cutters positioning the finger in between.

"Any last words? You can save the finger."

We're met with silence once again—no warning from Cole. Bolt cutters snap shut, and a finger drops to the floor, followed by a red river. Screams fill our tiny room. If you had asked me three years ago where I would be, I wouldn't have answered in a gang. I also didn't know my family would've kicked me out over doing drugs once, and if you're wondering, they live in Eastwood. I moved in with Cole, then Dorian moved in after a short period. They treated us like strangers of the town, so we became them. We joined Soul Stealers; it became our outlet then, and now I think we are all questioning Henry. His motives have gone out the window these last couple of months, more so weeks.

"Nyx, grab me a glove. I have something else to try." I don't question him anymore, and he's in his element. Good luck getting him out of it. Handing Cole a yellow rubber glove, I stand back and watch.

"If you're done screaming like a banshee, you can tell us anytime now." He slaps the glove on, bending down to pick up some feces. My gut turns, and Dorian gags. Cole shows a cruel smile on his lips as he draws his hand closer to dickhole's mouth.

Dickhole's eyes double in size when they see the feces in Cole's hand. "S-stop this p-please." Sweat drips down his trembling face.

"Then tell us, it's that simple, or this goes in your mouth." His voice matched the hardness of his gaze.

A pathetic whimper leaves his mouth. "I d-don't know." Cole moves closer. "I swear, it was done over the phone. We were told to be at that location. We weren't going to kill anyone. We were supposed to distract you three. That's all we were told."

Cold shivers race down my back. We left Catalina home alone for hours; something could've happened to her, and we would've gotten back in time. I'm pretty sure those gunshots were meant for us, not his men, as he told us. We better wrap this shit up so I can get to school, she may be safe there, but I'll feel a hell of a lot more relaxed with her in my sight.

"You have no names of who contacted you? Where did your men drive off to?" Dorian pushes for more answers.

But our guest has checked out, and the blood loss has taken over. I grab the smelling salts to wake his ass up. We aren't finished yet. He wakes with a jolt, smacking his head on the back of the chair.

"Talk some more fucker. Where are your men?"

"Gone. I ain't sayin' anything more."

I turn to the guys. "I'm done. I'm headed to the school to check on Cat. I'll see you at home?"

"Yeah, we're pretty much done here. I'll let Henry know it was for fun," Cole tells me, flicking the glove to the floor.

I leave, sending Cat a text letting her know I'm coming back. She wanted to do lunch, but my guts were still slightly unsettled with Cole's plans. He would've literally eaten shit and died. I almost gag, thinking that as I mount my bike. We were so close to finding who was after her. If only dickhole had more information for us. Now, she's never leaving my sight until he's caught. If he's already trying to set a plan in motion again, we have to be one step ahead of him this time.

I follow Cat into the driveway after school and want her on the back of my bike—one day. I pull open her door, waiting for her to gather her things. She gives me a beautiful smile when she steps out.

"Long time no see, handsome." Wrapping an arm around my waist, we head for the house.

"How was the rest of school?"

She shrugs. "The same. I have another art project due before the end of the term. I can't complain. That means Christmas break, and I'm really looking forward to a break from school."

Christmas. I can't think of that shit right now. Halloween was last week, wasn't it? "A break will be lovely, wouldn't it? You deserve all the rest in the world, baby." I press a kiss on the top of her head. Guiding her through the front door, we're greeted by the scent of rosemary. Dorian must be cooking a roasted chicken tonight for dinner.

"Mmm, smells amazing. I don't think I've eaten this well my entire life before." She kicked off the new boots that Dorian picked up for her, not without a fight from her. She wiggled her striped, socked toes at me, making me laugh.

"Come on, let's see what mom is cooking."

"He really is, isn't he."

Dorian and Cole are standing at the island when we walked in, drink in hand. It's not normal to see them drink. That's how I know today was a tough one for them. I study them, looking for signs of trouble, mainly if they talked to Henry. When I feel satisfied, I release Cat, and she moves toward Cole first. Reaching up on her tiptoes, she kisses his lips softly. When she turns away, he grabs her and presses into her again. I move towards the stove to see what is cooking. It was about time those two made up.

"How did it go?" I lean against the counter, looking at everyone. Dorian has Cat tucked under his arm now.

"As good as you can imagine. He didn't say anything after you left, so I finished the job. I went and found Henry to give him the full rundown. That was a fuckin' joke. That goddamn Conrad had to be there sticking his nose into everything we had to say." Cole scoffed, moving to the fridge. "Can you believe he tried to tell me how to torture someone to get information?" Slamming the door closed, he cracked open his beer. That would explain the drinking.

"Why would Conrad be sitting in on this meeting with Henry?"

"That's what I want to know. Next time he says something, I'm not biting my tongue."

I think we need a meeting with Henry alone to see what gives with this Conrad guy. I thought he was only here to find the grave digger. He technically did his job, so he should've left by now. We've been doing every job that Henry has given to us without a fight, even if it's stupid.

"Either way, we completed it. I'm not going to think about it. We still have more important shit to do."

"Yeah, like, catch my creepy kidnapper," Catalina adds.

We all gave her a cautious smile, a silent promise that we hoped to fulfill. We need a goddamn motive as to why he took her. Usually, a kidnapper leaves a note or at least calls. This person did nothing. He said nothing to her regarding why he was leaving us in the dark and no trail. Our only hope is if he makes another move, we better be around when he does.

"That's enough, suppers ready. We'll figure something out, but it won't be tonight." Dorian sets the food down on the table, motioning us to join. I'll have to agree. Without a game plan, we are sitting ducks.

"Supper looks wonderful. Thank you again for cooking."

Dorian cups her face. "Anything for you, darling." After dropping a kiss on her lips, he sits across from her. Cole parks his ass right next to her, grinning at me. Whatever, I'll let them have their time together.

"When are you going back to work, baby?"

She swallows her bite and wipes her mouth. "Actually, Dr. Deadbodies talked to me earlier about moving me to the lab. With the cooler months coming, he figured it would be better."

"That'll be all right then. Keep you in the warmth at least."

She gives me a slight shrug. "I don't enjoy working with other people, and they have a habit of casting me out before they get to know me." I see her side-eye, Cole. She hit the nail on the head with that one. He did a number on her.

"What's not to love about you? You're sarcastic, you aren't afraid to speak your mind, and best of all, you're great in bed." We all let out carefree laughs.

"Well, if anyone else gets you in bed, they'll have me to deal with," Cole declares.

Dorian and I both nod in agreement. Cat rolls her eyes.

"Don't worry, three cocks are all I can handle. Trust me. They just happen to be attached to three incredible guys I don't mind hanging around with."

"Wow, hanging around. You make it seem like we're all just friends," Dorian said.

"Well, I haven't been on a date yet. All we do is fuck, so you tell me, are we friends, or are we more?" She asked, her face unreadable.

I didn't know we had to take someone on a date these days to classify as a girlfriend, and I thought it was a given when we kept seeing each other. I look at the other two for help with an answer, but they look just as frustrated as me.

She can't help but crack up, and her body starts shaking from all the laughter bursting out of her mouth. "You... sshould've... sseen... your faces." She snorts, covering her mouth.

"You little witch." Cole goes in for the kill, tickling her sides and getting a shriek. She tries to get away from him, but he's too strong.

"Help me, Dorian."

"Nah, you have this coming half pint. You are ours, and no one else's understood?"

Cole stops pulling her onto his lap and nuzzles into her neck. "I understand," she moans.

With a tight grip on his shoulders, completely forgetting about dinner, he gets up from the table and strolls into the den. I look over at Dorian, who watches them leave. I jerk my chin in agreement, and we both follow after them.

Cole already has Cat's top off, caressing her breasts, her head tipped back, mouth open as she sends out a silent moan. Dorian walks behind her, working his hands under her skirt. I bit the inside of my cheek, and I do love it when she wears her skirts and leg harnesses.

"Take the skirt off, but leave the harnesses on," I told Dorian.

He does what I say, dropping her skirt to the floor, leaving her in nothing but her black thong, knee-high socks, and leather harnesses. Too bad she won't be getting completely naked tonight.

"Since you were a bad girl at supper, you need to be punished." I walk around her as Cole steps back.

"I'd have to agree. Tonight is all about us Wednesday. Get down on your knees and put that mouth of yours to work," Cole demands her, his inner dominance coming through.

She drops to her knees, waiting for our next move. My growing dick is pressing uncomfortably in my jeans. I step closer to her, and her hands quickly work, undoing my buttons. Her small hand wraps around my shaft as her other hand finds Dorian's cock. She strokes us at the same time while shifting her hips back and forth, looking for relief.

"Maybe you'll think twice about misbehaving?" Cole steps up, pumping his cock, and touching her lips. "Open." He slides in until she pulls back. He snaps his hand into her hair, pulling her back. She grips me tighter.

Spit slides down her chin with how hard Cole is fucking her. The room is filled with groans and slurping sounds. The sight of them together brings my release closer. Her hand hasn't let up once. Cole groans, going still.

"Don't you dare swallow." He backs away, letting me step in.

I take over for her. "Open, I'm coming." I pump a few more times, my muscles contracting as I come in her mouth. My cum and Cole's cum mix together. "Fuck, baby, that's hot."

Dorian is next. He doesn't give her a chance to close her mouth. He shoots his load right away, groaning loudly. "God, you're amazing."

"Now you swallow like a good girl," Cole told her.

I watch her throat work all of our cum down. I move her hair out of her face, kissing her deeply without a care in the world. "Do you think you deserve to come?"

"Yes," she whimpered. "Please, I need to come."

"Bend over then." She does what she is told. I slide her thong down, running my hands down her legs, barely touching her. Her pussy is dripping. "I love you in these." I run my hand over her leather harnesses.

"I know. That's why I wear them." She wiggles her ass, only for Cole to smack it. "Oh, fuck." He delivers another smack as my fingers enter her tight wet pussy. Dorian pinches her nipples. We all work together, bringing her an explosive orgasm. Her body is a trembling mess. She falls to the floor in a withering mess by the time we are done.

"Come on, baby, let's get you to bed." We have a busy day tomorrow. She mumbles something into my chest as I carry her to my bedroom. I lower her into bed, leaving a kiss on her forehead. I walk back downstairs to find the guys back in the kitchen.

"We need to find her kidnapper and soon. I have a plan, but you guys are not going to like it."

I fill them in on the plan, praying that it works.

8

CATALINA

Walking into Philosophy with Nyx feels different today. I can't place my finger on it, but something is off with him. Last night, he brought me to bed and cuddled with me closer than ever. I should've known then something was wrong. Even his looks give it away.

"Are you okay?" I grab his hand, intertwining our fingers together.

He tightens his fingers. "I'm good, don't worry. Just thinking about stuff with the gang, that's all." He gives me a tight smile, then turns back to our substitute professor.

They filled me in on what happened to Davis and Adams, and I owe them so much I need to find some time to visit them. No one else would've even thought twice about searching for me. To be honest, no one knows I exist besides three, no, I guess five people now.

"I have work tonight in the lab—no need to follow me home. I'm not sure how long I'll be. I've never done this before." I bite my lower lip, wondering how many people I'll have to talk to tonight.

"Hey, you'll be all right. Everyone will love you." He pulls me closer, leaning his forehead on mine.

I absorb his positive energy, trying to see how hanging around others will be good. "What if this blows up in my face?"

"Then we will be here to catch you, baby."

"Goes for you too, whatever's on your mind. I'm here for you." I gently kiss his lips before turning to face the front. I hear him groan and see him reposition himself.

The morning and afternoon dragged on, and I had nothing exciting happening in any of my classes. I was tempted to ditch out early to head to the lab but thought twice about it. I didn't want to be there longer than I needed to be. I also needed to find out why Nyx was acting so weird this morning, and I couldn't get it out of my mind all day. I tried texting him, but he left me unanswered. I assumed he was busy with classes. He was the only one who took schooling seriously. It was unlike him, though.

I decided to take a break and grab a bite to eat before going to the lab. I thought about asking the guys to join me but realized I needed some alone time. You know how it goes. They can get a little overwhelming, especially since being kidnapped by creepy jones. My baby was always waiting for me in the parking lot. I'm so glad she was fixed for me, running my hand along her black hood.

"Me and you for a while; let's go get some su—" Before I could finish my sentence, I noticed a yellow note under the wiper blade. With a shaky hand, I reach for it. I look around to make sure no one is around before unlocking the door. I have a feeling I know who this note is from. I'm not surprised it took this long for him to reach me. After sitting behind the wheel, I relock my door. With a deep, shaky inhale, I unfold the note.

Hello pretty girl,

I'm sure you're wondering why I waited so long to reach you, but all good things take time, as does my next move. The countdown begins now. Are you brave enough to find out on your own? Or will you need your three men to help you? Only time will tell. Tick tock, when will I strike again? Perhaps when a clock turns 12.

Until we meet again.

I refold the note, placing it in my bag. I stare at my bag like it's the plague now. What the hell does he want from me? Can't he at least give me that?

"Great, now what am I to do?" *Tell the guys.* I should be sending a mass text right now, so why am I not? In a way, I don't believe he'll be attacking me anytime soon. I just want one night to be normal without the guys breathing down my neck. Can't I have that, at least? I promise to tell them when I get home.

Driving to the small café, I lost most of my appetite since finding that note. I keep repeating the last sentence over and over. What day will it be and what twelve? Noon or midnight? The scary thing is, my creep could be anyone in this café. Without his mask on, he blends in so easily. I keep my eyes focused on the counter and quickly order my food to go. I'll eat in the car back on campus. That way, if a vehicle follows, I'll be able to spot it right away.

I grab my wrap and tea and leave. The streets are filling up with college kids leaving for the afternoon, everyone walking in groups chatting along without a care in the world. I'll have that soon—right? The drive back was uneventful, thankfully. I park right next to the back door under the light. I never noticed anyone following me, so maybe tonight isn't the night. That would be too convenient for him anyway, and he probably assumes I called the guys right away.

"You should've, dummy." They're going to be so mad. Luckily, I have hours before that happens. I shove the rest of my wrap in my mouth, gather up my garbage, and head inside. It's time to find out what all the fuss is all about working inside and with other people.

It turns out that working inside is only working with one other person, which isn't so bad. Riley works independently, so I don't have to talk to him like I thought I would. We've only exchanged about ten words so far. Two introverts working together are perfect. I also never thought I would be the person wearing a white lab coat, but here I am. I even sent a selfie to the guys. They all suddenly came down with a cold that needed a doctor to look them over. I threatened them with rectal temperatures in return. It's mostly filing and collecting data from the cadavers I brought in. I didn't think I would ever see the Joe's again. Seeing them lying on the medical table instead of inside the body bag is weird. I never told Riley that I was the one that brought them in. He figures the school orders them in for the students. Oh, poor innocent Riley. He wouldn't last a minute out in the cemetery with me.

"Hey, Catalina? Could you help me with something, please?" Riley doesn't bother looking up from his work, which is what it's been like since I started. He's earnest about his work.

"Um, yep. One second." I finish up with my typing before I forget every detail entirely. Thank God, I'm pretty decent on Excel, or I would be fucked right now. Sliding my chair over to Riley, I notice what he's working on. "Dude, I'm not helping with that."

"Why not? It's perfectly normal."

"Normal for whom?" He's elbow-deep in Joe's abdomen. I can honestly say I've never seen another person digging around in another before. I didn't think this was how it all went down.

He tilts his head to the side, giving me a smirk. His brown eyes illuminated under the light. "I have lived for this Catalina my entire life. I wanted to be worth something, and being here at this school, I finally can."

"You're worth more than you know, Riley, trust me." I pass him the kidney bowl as we get back to work. Neither of us speaks as we work simultaneously. You'd swear we've worked together for years. He's been a dream to work with, and I'll have to let Davis know I'm glad I took this job. Time flew by, and it was time to pack it up before I knew it.

"I'll see you later this week?" I ask while I grab my bag.

"You bet. I'll walk you out."

We both walk in the cool night. If I'm being truthful, I'm glad he walked me out. It's nearing midnight. My mood was slowly shifting to a damn near breakdown, and I needed to be somewhere private before that happened. He waves goodbye when I'm safely nestled inside Johnny. At full tilt, I speed out of that parking lot, trying to get home to my guys. I'm beating that clock no matter what. Tonight is not the night. No matter how often I told myself it wouldn't be happening tonight, I couldn't calm my nerves. My knuckles were white from gripping my steering wheel, and my heart jerked against its reins from all the adrenaline rushing through my body. Thankfully there weren't many people on the road because I was driving like someone ready to shit their pants. Trust me. I felt like I was.

The house came into view when I heard the sweet sound of a bike revving behind me. A grin sprang across my face. Of course, they would be watching my back even when I told them not to. They were pulling in behind me when I parked the car. I watched as they all dismounted their bikes. A pang of excitement hit me, waking up my hungry pussy. I have to bite my lip before I spill out my deep, dark fantasy as they walk closer to me. I damn near forgot why I was rushing home so quickly, for having them all around me staring at me like I'm their last meal calms me somehow.

"Fancy seeing you here." Nyx brushes his lips against mine before pressing them fully. Every time he kisses me, it's like he's leaving a piece of himself behind. He's the most thoughtful one. He knows exactly what I need without asking. This kiss is no different. He brushes my cheek before stepping back.

"Wednesday, how was work?"

I give Cole a half shrug. "Better than I thought, to be honest. Riley and I work really well together, so I can't complain."

He runs his hand along the back of my neck. "Is that so? Another man moving in on our woman?" He pulls me closer to him, tipping my head back. "You only have three men, remember that." Then he slams his lips on mine, taking all control. Cole always has to be in control, but I can taste his vulnerability. I tug him closer by his hoodie pocket.

"You're mine, all of you," I growl.

"Damn right, little one." I have to clench my thighs together to relieve some pressure on my throbbing clit.

"Fuck, I can smell how horny you are from here." Dorian comes up behind me, wrapping his arm around my waist and pushing me into his growing bulge. "Where's my kiss?"

I wrap my hand around his neck, pulling his head down to me as I tilt my head to meet his. Pressing my lips against his sends shock waves down my body. This tall, muscular man may be gentle, but he'll do filthy things to me. His hands slip lower on my stomach, resting just above my waistband. I pull away breathlessly, closing my eyes. I can either tell them about the letter or strip them all naked. My head says one thing, and my slutty pussy is screaming the other thing.

"I have to tell you, guys, something important." I look at them, feeling nervous. "Inside, though."

Cole's gaze hardens instantly. "What happened?"

I can only shake my head. Dorian wraps both arms around me, directing me towards the house. I got this. I can tell them without breaking down, and it's not that bad. I have them for strength and support.

What could go wrong?

9

DORIAN

Catalina is pacing the den, and I swear she's going to wear the floor out. When she told us she had something to say, I knew it was serious, but it couldn't be good for her to be stressed like this.

"Just take a deep breath. We're here for you. Lean on us." Nyx gently coaxes her.

She gives him a ghost of a smile, and that's when it hits me.

"Did he find you again?" I rise out of my seat and rush towards her. Bringing her into a tight hug. She nods her head. "Fuck, half pint. Why didn't you call?" I pick her up and walk back to my chair, and she curls into my body, looking at the other two.

"Tell us Wednesday. I'm going crazy here, and I need to know who to kill." Cole's fists clench and unclench in his lap.

"That's the thing, and I still don't know." She buries herself closer to me, needing comfort more than anything. "He left me a note on my car. It's in my bag if you want to read it. He didn't say much. Everything is all on the note, though."

Nyx goes for her bag, digging around until he finds a yellow folded piece of paper. I watch him as he reads it. He goes from his calm self to someone who would burn the world down. His eyebrows pinch in the middle of his forehead as he passes the note to Cole.

"The fuck, Catalina. How long have you been holding onto this?" His voice is laced with so much hatred, either towards her or her fucking stalker.

When he passes it to me, she finally answers. "I found it as I left school earlier, mid-afternoon."

What I read leaves me disgusted. This piece of shit violated her again and is now taunting her and leaving just enough clues that he's planning something but won't fully come out and say something. We need to find him. I know Nyx has a plan; he gave us a few details last night after we placed her in bed, but we now have to execute it fully. It was a good thing we followed her home tonight. If he were going to pull something, we would've been close by to save her.

"Why didn't you call or text one of us?" I question her, placing the note on the arm of the chair. "We would've been there in a heartbeat."

I could tell she didn't want to answer me. I rub her back, letting her know we're here no matter what. We won't be leaving just because she didn't need us.

"I figured he would be stupid to pull his plan off tonight, especially when he just delivered his note. He probably thought I called one of you. I wanted to, but in a way, I also wanted to handle this on my own. I'm sorry."

"Don't apologize. Call next time. This is serious. He still could've tried something, and we need to take everything he says seriously from now on," I told her.

Nyx moves closer, placing a hand on her thigh. "We're serious, baby. We can't lose you again. This guy didn't care about anything and didn't try anything until now to leave you a message out of the blue. That scares the fuck out of me."

"Same, and hardly anything scares me." Cole walks around me, placing a kiss on her forehead. "Don't fuckin' pull that shit again, or I'll have to punish you." She shifts on my lap, and I watch her swallow harshly. I suddenly remember something from earlier in the driveway. We should finish up before I strip her naked.

"One of us will always be with you from now on, either on the bike or in your car. You will not be travelling alone. You eat with us. When twelve o'clock comes around, all of us are with you." We all wait for her to say something. This is huge for her. I know how much she likes to have her space.

She closes her eyes and reaches out her hand, waiting for any of us to grab it. Nyx intertwines his fingers with hers. "I understand why you guys always want to attach yourself to me, but you really don't need to. You have a life, too, and a gang to help with. You can't stretch yourselves thin."

"Don't you dare worry about us. We can handle it. There are three of us. Tag teaming is what we do well." Cole kisses down her neck, making her grind into my dick. I have to grip her waist tight to hold her still.

A groan slips past my lips as she grinds harder. I guide my hands under her shirt, touching her soft skin. I'll never get enough of her. She drives me crazy. She moans when Cole runs his hand around her neck.

"Tell us what you want." He uses his thumb to tilt her chin to the side. Lowering his face to hers, he plants small kisses along her jawline.

Breathlessly, she tells us. "I want all three of you at once, please. I want to feel only my men tonight."

Cole walks away, heading towards the desk, while I move her onto the couch. Nyx is already stripping his clothes. I pull her shirt off, leaving her in a pink lace bra.

"So beautiful. How did I get so lucky?"

She runs her hands through my hair, staring into my eyes. "The question is, how did I get so lucky? You're one of a kind, Dorian. You may look like you'll beat everyone up, but you're gentle with me."

I let out a husky laugh. "That's because you're half my size. I'd squish you if I weren't."

"Whatever." She smacks me in the arm, but I barely feel it since she's smaller than me.

I love how we can easily joke, even during the most intimate times; it wouldn't work out if we took everything so seriously. I need some carefree time in my life, and I'm so grateful she's the one to bring it. I pull her leggings down slowly, almost painfully kissing her thigh as I go. Her laugh turns to a moan, then a whimper when I pull away completely.

Cole finally comes back, holding something in his hand. "Can we try something? You can say no and use your safe words if you have to."

When I get a good look, I see its leather cuffs. My stomach sinks at the thought of her having a panic attack, but when I turn to her, I don't know any form of stress.

"I'll try for you guys. Red is my safe word," she says with determination. Nyx caresses her inner thigh, distracting her somewhat from Cole. He helps her sit up before removing her bra. Cole moves her hands behind her back, letting her back out still. When she doesn't, he places one cuff on.

"How does that feel?"

She nods. "Good, I'm good." She releases a breath. "You can continue."

He caresses the inside of her right wrist before placing the other cuff on, immobilizing her. "Still feeling good?"

Her breath hitches when he tugs at it. "I'm good."

I stand, gripping my shirt at the back of my neck. I pull it over my head, she tries to shift closer to me, but with her hands behind her back, she's having a hard time. I take pity and move forward. Her lips land on my stomach before licking upwards. I wrap my hand in her hair, bringing her face higher.

"Want something else to lick?"

"Yes, please."

I undo my pants with one hand, pulling out my hard dick for her. I guide her head back down, waiting for her warm, wet mouth to take me in. I'm almost ready to lose myself when she hollows her cheeks, sucking me harder. I pull out, caressing her face, taking in her beauty. Before I get lost in her looks, I sit on the couch, letting Nyx move in.

"Hey, baby." He cups her face stealing a kiss from her, not caring that she was just sucking my dick seconds before. He strokes himself before brushing the tip over her lips. "Suck me as you've missed me." When she opens, he enters ever so slowly. She bobs her head, taking him all the way. She does this by getting a low groan from Nyx. Cole moves closer, getting on his knees and pulling her legs apart. Her pussy is so wet it's sticking to the sides of her thighs.

"Mmm, little one. Are you getting ready for us?" He throws a leg over his shoulder, getting his face nice and close to her aching pussy. The second Cole makes contact with his tongue. She makes a mumbled moan.

"Oh... fuck that feels good. Don't stop." Her hips move against Cole's face, and Nyx moves out of the way so Cole can shift onto the floor, taking Cat with him. "Sit on my face, little one." She kneels over his face, and he lets out a growl. "I said sit, not hover." He grips her hips and pulls her down. She lets out a scream followed by a moan. She tilts her head to the ceiling, eyes clamped shut as Cole eats her out.

I notice the bottle of lube on the couch. Placing some on my finger, I move behind her. I run my finger over her tight hole. While Nyx pinches her nipple, getting her to relax. When my finger is fully inside, her fingers tighten into a fist. I gently kiss her back, and she lets out a greedy moan. Adding more lube, I slide in a second finger.

"Yes, baby, take him. Let Cole eat you out. Fuck, you look so hot right now."

"Such a good girl, aren't you." I can feel her inner muscles tighten around my fingers. I pump my fingers more, and her body grows stiffer, her breathing coming in faster.

"Don't stop. I'm right there!" she screams. Her toes curl, and her hands ball into tight fists. When she's finished milking my fingers, I withdraw them. Kiss her back when she slumps forward. Nyx catches her before she hits the floor. Cole moves her to the side, face covered in her wetness. I unclip her wrist, letting her arms free.

"You did amazing, baby." Nyx places a kiss on her forehead. "Got any more energy?"

"Always." She smiles at him.

I move back to the couch, waiting for her. When she crawls over, I have to grip myself. She looks sexy, looking up at me between my legs. She licks her lips and takes over, stroking me. I let out a hiss from her touch. Her small hand doesn't even close around my thick dick.

"Get up here. I want that pussy." She straddles me, and my dick jumps when her pussy brushes against it. My hands tighten around her waist, pulling her closer to me. My lips press against hers, tasting her need. I lift my hips, stretching her with my smooth head. "Fuck," I mumble as soon as I push inside. I dip my head, taking her tight nipple in my mouth. She rocks her hips, moaning when she finds her motion. Another set of hands appears on her waist. When I look up, I grin at Nyx.

"This ass, baby. I'm dying to fuck it again."

"It's... yours." She moans.

I bring her closer to my chest, letting Nyx get better access to her ass. Holding her still, he pushes inside. The fullness of having him inside is almost too much, and we thrust, alternating our movements.

"Oh, fuck. It's so much."

Cole moves next to her, taking her hand to his dick. She takes him into her mouth. He wraps her hair around his hand, pressing her further onto his dick. She gags when he touches the back of her throat, and he doesn't let up. He holds her there until drool falls from her mouth. She takes a deep breath when he pulls out, only to do it again. All while Nyx and I push further into her pussy and ass. I run my hand over her sensitive bud, flicking it with my thumb, and she squeezes her inner walls.

Cole releases her. "I'm not coming unless it's inside that pussy. Now come for them, little one."

She lets out a small whimper. I thrust deeper and rub her clit in fast circles. Cole pinches her nipple, sending her over the edge. Her nails dig into my shoulders as she comes around us.

"Fuck, baby. Squeeze me harder." Nyx drives in harder in her ass as I pull out of her pussy. When I push back into her pussy, I feel her clamp around us.

My dick thickens, shooting my cum deep inside her. I groan into her neck, and I can feel Nyx grow thicker moments later, going still as he finishes in her ass. He lowers his head on her back. We take a breather until Cole speaks.

"Get that pussy over here now before I slap it."

She clenches around us, and we groan. Our woman loves dirty talk, especially from Cole. Nyx gently slides out of her, causing her to whimper.

"Did I hurt you?" He looks at her with concern.

"No, you were amazing." She winks at him before moving to Cole.

Cole, standing at the end of the couch, she doesn't even wait to be told what to do. She bends over with her ass in the air. With one quick smack on her ass, she spread her legs for him. He lines up and slams inside of her. He always did fuck like there was no tomorrow.

"Don't you ever hold information back from us again?" Another smack on her ass cheek. She moans louder, pushing back into him. If I hadn't come already, the sight of both of them would throw me over the edge. The sound of skin smacking against each other, moans, and grunts fills the room.

He digs his fingers into her hips more when he reaches for her arm, folding it behind her back and grabbing her other one before locking the handcuffs together. He grabs hold of it tight before pumping harder, and a light sheen of sweat covers her skin.

"Cole, I need to come," she whines.

"When… *thrust*… I… *thrust*… say… *thrust*… so." He doesn't let up, even when her legs shake.

He pulls out, turning her over with her ankles over his shoulders. Pushing back in her, she closes her eyes, biting her lip.

He runs his finger between her slit. "Come for me, little one." She explodes around him.

Her scream goes horse after a few seconds, and he finally goes, still grunting his release inside her. We're all silent as they come back to us. He releases her legs, working quickly to remove the cuffs from her. Nyx comes into the room with a cloth ready to clean her. I have a blanket when she's ready to be covered. We worked her extra tonight.

"You did so well, baby. Let us take care of you now." She mumbles her answer, eyes already heavy with sleep. I'm glad we could take things off her mind so she could sleep tonight.

Cause come tomorrow, it'll be walking into the unknown.

10

COLE

I'm sitting in the kitchen the next morning, rereading the note that Catalina was kindly left. I'm looking for a hidden clue or anything to go on. I take another sip of my coffee, wondering how we are going to catch this guy. Nyx's plan was smart, but now we don't need to worry about catfishing a lunatic.

"What are you doing up so early?" Nyx's smooth voice breaks the quietness of the morning. I watch as he moves to the counter to pour a cup of coffee.

"Couldn't sleep. This stupid note has been eating away at me." I toss the note back on the table.

He takes one glance at it, shaking his head. "I get it. We'll find him. Hopefully soon. I have a feeling it'll end in our favour and in our favourite room."

"Very optimistic of you."

He slumps in the chair across from me. "Have to be, and I don't want to think about any other outcome. Plus, it took us how long to get her. Finally, I'm not jeopardizing shit, man."

I understand this completely, especially after the way I treated her. I still had no right to be with her. I will always blame myself for everything that happens to her.

"You have to stop blaming yourself, and I can see it written all over your face."

"What do you expect from me?" I get up, walk towards the fridge, and need a breather. I always hated to be confronted with problems I couldn't control, and Catalina was one of them.

"Cole, if she doesn't hate you, then it's not a problem. Stop trying to fix something that isn't broken."

I stare inside the fridge, looking for help. "What if I'm not good enough for her?"

"Well, I say that's bullshit. Because I think you are the most honourable person I know. So how about you stop thinking for me." Her gentle voice was strong yet determined to put me in my place. She stood in the kitchen's doorway, looking unamused yet still sexy as fuck.

Dorian comes up behind her, hugging her. "Pay no attention to him, darling. He only speaks bullshit anyway. Come on, and I'll make breakfast before school."

"I'd fuckin' say he speaks bullshit. If any of you second guess my relationship between us, I'll kick your asses."

I have to laugh and wave my hand in the air. "Remember what happened last time you tried to hurt me?"

She screwed up her nose. "That's because you're all fuckin' giants compared to me. It's not fair."

"What you lack in height, you make up in attitude, and I love that in you." I place a kiss on her lips, sucking on her bottom lip between my teeth, nibbling lightly before letting go. I smack her on the ass before walking to where Dorian is prepping breakfast. I hear her groan as she sits down.

Nyx drove with her to school while Dorian and I followed in the truck. We would've taken the bikes, but we felt we blended into traffic better this way. We usually never drive the truck to school, so if he was watching her, he didn't know what to look out for. I pulled into the far lot overlooking her car.

"Everything up and running?"

Dorian grunts at the lack of head space between the windshield and the dash. "Yeah, if anything happens, this should catch it. He shouldn't suspect a thing."

"Good, let's do this. Henry has a job for us later, too, so we need to time it correctly that we are home by midnight, or at least one of us is home."

He rolls his eyes as he steps out. I feel the same way. We can't be slacking on our duties, though. We signed up for this shit, after all. The walk toward campus was stressful, and we weren't aware of what he looked like. He could be any one of these douchebags walking around. The scary thing is he knows who we all look like, my nickname for her. I'm hoping he hasn't figured out where we live yet. I scan every direction until I'm inside and can hug Cat.

"Be safe until lunchtime, I swear to God. I will burn this school down if I have to." Her small hands cupped my face.

"Cole, you need to worry less. I can see grey hair already." She tries to bite back a laugh.

I place my hands over hers. "That's not funny," I growl closer to her face. "You're asking for a sore-ass little one." I watch her shift slightly, and I back away with a smirk.

"Jerk," she mumbled. She and Nyx walk toward their philosophy class. I'll be able to breathe a little easier for the next couple of hours. She'll be with him or Dorian.

Dorian and I go our separate ways, and I head to my lame English lit class that I've never paid attention to. Whether I graduate or not isn't a big deal to me. Henry's paying either way, so what did it matter to me? I didn't want to be here. This class felt like it dragged. Who wanted to learn about old dead writers for two hours? I'm itching to get the fuck out of this stuffy room, and I need to make sure she's okay. I sent a text to Nyx, but all he sent back was a stupid thumbs-up emoji. How the hell am I supposed to know what that means?

It's thirty minutes until twelve. I've come to the cafeteria early to find a table where we can sit and view the entire room. I'm not chancing dickshit today. I'm watching every entrance when Dorian walks in. He does a quick scan when he sees me. He heads to the line. I get a ding on my phone, letting me know he'll grab everyone's food. I wait patiently for the only person I need right now. Moments later, I hear her laugh before I see her. The second my eyes land on her, hers turn toward mine. Even in the crowded room, she finds me.

"Hey, you. How was class?" She throws her bag on the floor, coming to sit next to me.

I wrap my arm around her shoulder, pulling her closer to me. "I hate school. I would quit if I could." I kiss her on the temple. "How was your morning?"

"The usual packed solid. I have that art project I need to finish or really start. I've been slacking a lot lately."

The aroma hits me hard, and Dorian chooses that time to drop food off. I pass her a pop and then a piece of pizza. She dives in like she's been starving for years. It's only been a couple of hours since breakfast.

"Slow down, baby. You'll choke."

She sticks her tongue out at Nyx, then chews. "What's the plan after school? I need to run by a drugstore to grab a few supplies your house lacks for a woman. I also need to stop by my place sometime this week for more clothes."

"You have Nyx for the rest of the day. Dorian and I have a job to do." It was the only thing I could think of without leaving anyone short-handed. Henry gets his job done. She's not left alone. I see him wiggle his eyebrows at her. Lucky asshole.

"Just stay safe. I'll see you when we get home." Dorian stands behind her, rubbing her shoulders.

"Don't worry about me, big guy. I have my bear spray that I won't drop this time, plus Nyx will protect me, and if he sticks to his note, it's only midnight now that he'll attack."

He closes his eyes. "Still. Get in the house before then. We should be home by then, anyway." He leans down, kissing her forehead. He glances at me from the corner of his eye.

We better be home by then.

Conrad greets us as we walk into the warehouse.

"Hello, gentlemen. I'll be working with you tonight. Henry wanted me to get a lay of the gang that includes you three—you're missing one." He looks around for Nyx like he's going to appear magically.

"Yeah, he sends his regards, but he has an assignment due, and if you know Nyx, he takes his school very seriously." I shrug, walking past him toward Henry's office.

"Ah, well. I'll remember that. Always good to have a well-educated man working for us."

There he goes again, including himself in the gang. Henry needs to clarify some bullshit for us. Speaking of the cunt, he's sitting at his desk smoking, looking extra cozy, knowing he doesn't have to lift a finger tonight. This better not be another scam.

"Perfect timing, sit. I need to tell you all something. Where's Nyx? This includes him, too."

"Schoolwork." That is all I say when I sit resting my ankle over my knee. Dorian takes the seat next to me, sitting with his legs stretched out, looking comfortable but on guard.

Conrad takes Henry's side and grabs a glass of whiskey. I try to keep my face neutral, but this smells fishy.

"I have a job for you, but I have some exciting news. Since Conrad has come on board, I've been stepping back and letting him take the reins," Henry starts.

News to me: he captures the wrong people, and you suddenly trust him more.

"I'm thinking of making him the acting VP. Since we've never had one before, but I do give out roles in this gang, might as well have a VP, right? If something were to happen to me, I thought it would be good to have things in order. What do you think?" he looks at me.

I run my hand through my hair, blowing out a breath. Does he want me to answer that?

"I think it's complete fucking bullshit. You're going to ask someone you know for what, a week compared to, say, Cole, that you've known for years. Fuck that shit." Dorians' voice shook with fury.

I guess he got his answer.

"Thank you, boy, but I wasn't asking you."

Dorian jolts upright, getting in his face. "Fuck you, fuck this gang. It's for pussies." He spits on Henry's desk. I dart up fast, grabbing the back of Dorian's shirt.

"Do you know what you're saying? If you want out, that means I still owe all three of you. That precious schooling that Nyx loves so much. I'll cut him off."

"Try it. I fuckin' dare you. Dorian and I are done with school, but Nyx is not. This gang doesn't deserve us, and you know it. Either figure that out, or we're out for good."

That could've gone a better fuckin' way, Goddamnit. We both walk out in silence. I'm trying to figure out how to explain all of this to Nyx when we get home earlier than expected. If we leave the gang, I have a good chunk of money saved. I can pay for Nyx without him noticing.

"Sorry about that. I can't stand being called a boy," Dorian says, slamming the truck door closed.

I clasp my hand on his shoulder. "I know. It's not your fault. That was sprung on us like a fart turning into shit. I didn't expect him to give Conrad everything if he kicked the bucket. What's up with that?"

He rubs his temples. "Think he just wants to go legit with the gang? Make it bigger than what it already is?"

"You mean to move from a gang and into an MC?"

He nods. He could be, *fuck,* he already technically made us the enforcers and calls himself the president. He wanted everyone living around the warehouse like one big family. He could be, for all I know, still. He could've tried doing it differently.

"Let's go home and surprise the shit out of those two."

"They are probably already halfway naked by now."

I fire up the truck, heading home. If they are naked, I'm joining in.

11

CATALINA

I've been stressing all day, and my gut was telling me something was going to happen. I knew it was wrong. Noon has come and gone without a hitch. Nyx and I are currently walking the halls of EU and heading to my next class. Unfortunately, our classes are at opposite ends, so our goodbye is relatively quick.

"Stay inside until I grab you." He treads his hands in my hair, tugging my head back, his green eyes meeting mine.

"I know. You've told me a million times already. Trust me. I'm not leaving without you."

He tugs my hair harder; I hold back a moan. Now's not the place for this, although flashes of what we did in school weeks ago go through my mind, and I smile.

"Baby, get those dirty thoughts out of that head. You go to class." He places a quick kiss on my lips. "I'll be back in an hour to fetch this pretty ass."

I reach up on my tiptoes, pressing my lips to his. "I'll miss you."

"Miss you too."

He waited until I was in my class before he walked away. I turn to watch him walk away, getting a glimpse of his ass. I still don't know how I got to be so lucky. I find my seat, prepared to be bored for over an hour.

I'm watching the clock. Every second that passes is another second closer to getting out of this place. You'd swear I was doing time in maximum security, and my parole was coming up. I'm tapping my pencil on my paper, fixated on that damn clock. I don't know why. The professor can hold us longer if they choose to.

"Miss. Wilson." I have no idea why I'm even watching it. This professor is kind of a dick, anyway.

"Miss. Wilson." I continue to tap my pencil when it's suddenly ripped out of my hand. I look up to a very pissed off professor. I send him a nervous smile.

"Can I help you?" I ask.

"You can, by listening and paying attention, or you can leave the class. It doesn't matter to me. I get paid either way."

What did I tell you, dick.

"Can I have my pencil back, please?"

He blew his nostrils wide, narrowing his eyes at me. "Smarten up, Miss. Wilson, I won't give you another warning." He passes me back my pencil. I grab it, pulling it towards me when he doesn't let go. We pull in opposite directions, I let go first, and his arm flings backwards.

"I don't need it, and I have a spare." I give him a smirk before facing the front. I have a feeling I'm not passing this class anytime soon. After giving me a stink eye, he walks away. I can feel eyes on me. I don't dare look around. I hardly ever bring attention to myself. What has gotten into me?

When the asshole professor finally releases us, Nyx is leaning against the wall across the hall. His long legs crossed at the ankles, his nose stuck in a book. He hasn't noticed that I've been secretly drooling over him yet. When he does look up, he shoots me the brightest smile.

"Hey, baby." He closes his book, tucking it back into his back. "If you're done drooling, we can head out."

My mouth drops open. "I was so not drooling." I retort. I walk away, wiping my lips just in case.

"I saw that," he hollered from behind me.

"You didn't see nothin'. Hurry up, hotshot." I turn around, skipping backwards, feeling happy. The smile on his face also makes me happy. I stop dead in my tracks. When he finally catches up to me, I grab his hand. "Nyx, you really are a kind person, you know that, right?" He raises one eyebrow in confusion. "I didn't think I would find myself in this kind of relationship, especially after everything went down between us." I cup his cheek, lifting on my tiptoes. My lips skimming his. "I love you so much."

His eyes shine bright. "I love you too, baby." His lips press against mine, letting me feel all his love. This is what I've been missing all my life. I've never felt anyone's love before. He pulls me off my feet, swinging me in a circle. A small laugh falls out of my mouth.

"You're crazy, Nyx Thornton."

"Crazy for you. Come on. We have things to get done before the others get back."

⸎

You know what's not fair, being a girl. It's crazy expensive, especially in this small ass town. Throwing the box of tampons in my basket, I search for pain meds, nothing worse than bleeding, but let's add cramps on top of that.

"Fucking bullshit."

"What is?"

I jump at the sound of Nyx's voice. I tilt my head back to see him towering over me. "Being a girl, buddy. It's complete bullshit. Can I borrow your dick sometimes, and you take the uterus?"

"No can do. I'm rather attached to little Nixie." He readjusts himself to prove it.

I roll my eyes, tossing the pain meds in the basket. While we were cashing out, I noticed a sign on the counter.

"I didn't know the clock was broken. When did that happen?" I slip my debit card out to pay.

The cashier says, "Oh, that happened shortly after Halloween or that night. Probably a bunch of kids, to be honest. The construction crew will block the road, so I'd advise you to go around the park so you don't get stuck in traffic."

"Thanks, we will. Have a great day," Nyx tells her with a smile.

I take my items and head for the door. "Well, that's a shame about the clock. It was so old. Stupid kids always have to ruin everything, don't they?"

His hand falls on the small of my back as he guides me to Johnny. "That they do. We should've considered watching over Main Street more instead of going to the cemetery." He smiles down at me.

"Nah, the cemetery was a perfect choice." I laugh.

We had to park down the street. The parking is outrageously busy today. It's like everyone did all of their Christmas shopping today. A chill runs down my back, and Nyx pulls me closer to his side. But even his warmth can't get rid of this chill. I feel eyes on me. It could be in my head since my creeper isn't caught yet. I relax a little when my car comes into view. I'm digging the keys out of my pocket when I hear Nyx let out a quiet hiss sound. I look at him, noticing he's stiffened up, furrowing my brows. I step away from him.

That's when I saw him. His hood is over his head, casting a dark shadow over his features. His hand is pressed into Nyx's back, and things are taking a while to slowly register why he isn't walking away from the creep. When they do, I try to reach for the bear spray in my bag.

"Don't even, pretty girl. That bear spray won't work, or I'll shoot your boyfriend or one of them, I should say."

I halt my movements. I'm not placing Nyx in danger. It's me he wants. "You said noon or midnight. It's neither of them." I keep my voice steady, even though all I want to do is cry.

He tsks at me. "No, you didn't read my note correctly."

"Bullshit, we didn't," Nyx spits out. He lets out another hiss when creep presses the gun harder into his back.

"You didn't, and I said when a clock says twelve. If you look at the town clock, I do believe it's set too—." He lets his sentence die off.

I already have a feeling what the clock says, and it's doomsday. My time is up. Everything we did didn't matter in the end.

"What do you want from her? You had her once and did fuckin' nothing with her, you pathetic loser." Nyx doesn't see the hit coming for him, and before I can warn him, a fist contacts with the side of his face.

"Stop, please. I'll do anything you want. Just leave him alone," I beg like my life doesn't matter. Right now, it doesn't. I need Nyx to get away. *"Please."*

My creep takes another deep breath. "You still don't get it, do you? You aren't important. You never were. Even after all these years, you still won't go away."

What the hell does that mean? He said I was impor-tant. Was it all a mind game? Before he can answer, Nyx turns so quickly, tackling him to the ground. I'm so busy watching them fight I forget we are in the middle of the sidewalk. The clattering of metal next to me makes everything come crashing down.

"Cat, call the guys now."

My hands fumble in my bag, and my mind has flash-backs to that night I ran from him in the school parking lot. I'm not alone this time. My guys are with me this time. I find Cole's name in my phone and hit call. I watch as Nyx and creep continue to fight. I kick the gun further away, waiting for Cole to answer his fucking phone.

"Hey, Wednesday. I thought you would be balls deep with Nyx by now," He lets out a deep laugh. His deep voice should bring me comfort, but it doesn't.

"Cole." I gasped out.

"Catalina, what is it." All laughter dies in his voice.

"He found us. We're on Main Street. please hurry." My voice shakes. I'm more worried about Nyx than I am about myself.

"We'll be there soon. Hold tight." The phone goes dead before I can say the words I've been meaning to say for a while now.

I glance back at Nyx to see him sitting on top of the creeps back, with his knee in his back and his arms re-strained.

"What did Cole say?"

I shake my head. Right, Cole. "They'll be here soon, that's all he said. What are we gonna do with him?" I keep my distance, even though I really want to see who he is.

"Go sit in the car and wait. Lock the doors."

"I'm not leaving you." I shake my head, determined not to listen to him.

"Baby, please. Listen to me this one time," he grunts as the creep fights him again.

I walk backwards, never taking my eyes off them. My hand reaches back until it hits my car door, fumbling until I find the handle. I don't want to leave Nyx alone, but he doesn't give me a choice. I can only pray that the guys show up before something happens.

My eyes don't leave them for a second. I don't trust that creep at all. My phone rings, and I damn near jump out of my skin.

"Hello." I nervously answered. I didn't bother to check who called.

"Half pint, where are you?"

God, that husky voice. "Dorian, I'm in my car. Where the hell are you guys?"

"We're stuck in traffic, the fucking construction we didn't know about."

Oh, fuck. I completely forgot about that. My entire body wants to shrivel up. I turn to see Nyx struggle with the creep more and more.

"You need to hurry. What am I supposed to do?"

Nyx is thrown off the creep's face. I need to do something. I fling open my car door without thinking. I ignore Dorian yelling at me through the phone and run towards Nyx.

He needs me.

Just as I'm about to fling myself into the creep's body, he suddenly pulls down the hood. I lose my balance and fall to my knees, dropping my phone in shock. My hands fly to my mouth as tears well up in my eyes. The realization hits me like a ton of bricks. I had known who it was all along.

"How could you?" My voice shakes. My body wants to crawl in on itself.

"It wasn't personal—wait, it is," he recalls, tapping his chin.

Nyx looks complex. He doesn't know what to do. "Baby, you know this asshole?"

I close my eyes and slowly nod. Taking a deep breath, I turn towards the person I thought I wouldn't see again.

"I do. This is my older brother."

My brother, or as I like to refer to him as her older son, starts laughing.

"Haven't changed, have you? Momma was right about you. Such a slut aren't you."

Nyx's fist darts out fast, punching my mother's son in the face.

He laughs. "You always needed someone to fight your fights for you, didn't you?"

"What the hell do you need? Why did you come find me?" I'm getting tired of him darting around my questions. I've had two years of freedom from that family. Why now did he come find me?

"Turns out Daddy Dearest loved you more than you thought." He rolls his eyes.

Two dark shadows cast alongside me, bringing me more strength to face the person who was supposed to be my friend growing up, the person who should've had my back, not beating me when my mother told him to. That's not what siblings are supposed to do.

I take a deep breath, willing myself not to break down.

"What does that mean? He didn't care my entire life."

He scoffs. I can feel Dorian stiffen alongside me. "Tell yourself what you need to. In the end, he left you every fuckin thing."

Cole places his hand on my shoulder. "What?" My mind is having a hard time playing catch up.

"God, you're fucking slow. Too many hits when you were younger. Father's dead. He left you everything, and I came to collect, except you are needed alive."

I sway on my feet, and Cole's grip tightens. "So, you stalk and kidnap me?"

He shrugs. "I figured I'd scare you a little before I tell you the truth."

"Are you fucking kidding me!" Dorian screams thunderously. Cole had to move to hold him back.

I'm at a loss for words. Why would my father leave anything to me? He did nothing my entire life to stop my mother and her ways. Was it the guilt that he felt, or was this some sick joke of his that he was playing? Let's stick it to Catalina and give one last final hurrah from the grave and give her some hope, only to take it away. Well, jokes on you. I don't want anything from that family anymore.

"Stop it. I can't do it anymore. Whatever he left me, just take it. I don't want it. I only wanted his help when Mother would make you beat me. Even then, he wouldn't help me, and I don't want his help now. Take it and leave me alone. Never look for me again."

Her son has a huge smirk on his face, like he just won the lottery. Maybe he did. I don't want to know what was left to me. "I'll get the lawyer to send the paperwork over and sign it, or I'll be back, Catalina."

He walks away, leaving me alone with my men.

12

CATALINA

I watch him walk away, all over some stupid inheritance that I didn't even ask for or want. I honestly didn't think my father had any money, and we didn't live as we did. Although my mother thought she should've been treated like the queen, she thought she was.

"Come on, baby, let's head home. It's been an eventful day." Nyx comes up, bringing me into a hug. I take in his spice and citrus smell. So glad he was with me today. "Love you."

"Love you too," I say into his chest.

"Wednesday, can we talk?"

"Now? Can't we talk at home?" I'm trying not to come off whiny, but I can't help it. I'm tired and want to curl up on the couch and relax with all three of them.

"Trust me, please." He reaches for my hand. "We'll catch up with you guys later."

He steers us toward his truck. We don't talk as we walk. He holds my hand the entire time, letting me know he's here for me. Once inside the cab, the first tear finally falls. I would blame it on PMS, but that bitch comes with a vengeance. This is for freedom. I'm finally free from my family once and for all.

"Hey, baby, what's wrong?" Cole brings me into his strong arms. His woodsy scent has always been my favourite smell. I cling to his shirt.

"I'm having a hard time with this, in a good way. He could've gone another way to get his stupid money. But it wouldn't be like him if he didn't torment me one last time, you know?" I wipe away my tears. I take a deep breath and pull away from him. "Sorry, you wanted to talk, and here I am, being a crying baby." I let out a small laugh.

He runs his thumb over my cheek, wiping another tear away. "Don't you dare apologize for any of this. I was so scared when you called. I can't lose you, Catalina." He lowers his lips to mine, kissing me so softly I could cry all over again. "I love you with all my heart and would give up the world for you."

I close my eyes, absorbing all of his love. I kiss him deeper, running my hands through his hair. He lets out a low moan. "I love you too, Cole Valentine," I whisper over his lips. "Now, take me home."

Dorian's in the kitchen cooking, and Nyx is lying on the couch when we walk in. This feels right. Now that I'm not in danger anymore, I can finally move back to my apartment. Even thinking about moving back in turns my stomach. I'm so used to being around these three that it'll be lonely again. I leave Cole and Nyx to seek my muscled man.

The kitchen is omitting a beautiful aroma. "Oh, my god. What's cooking stud muffin?" I make a show of wiping my mouth and getting a hearty laugh from Dorian.

"Nothing special, homemade burgers and fries."

I come up behind him, wrapping my arms around his waist. "Comfort food, exactly what I need. Thank you for everything you do, Dorian. I don't tell you that enough, and I'm sorry for that." He whips around so fast, gripping my chin.

"No. I need to apologize. I treated you like shit for a very long time, and I'll continue to grovel no matter what day it is. You are too special, not too." His blonde hair flops over his forehead, and I push it out of the way, his green eyes piercing into mine.

"I love you beyond the years, Dorian Prescott. You make me feel like I'm home."

"Fuck me, half pint. I've never heard those sweet words before. I can't believe you chose me to love." He caresses my cheek. "I love you, darling, for all the tomorrows. My life is complete with you in it."

His lips finally meet mine. I fist his t-shirt, moaning when his tongue dips into my mouth, swiping over my tongue. My pussy throbs with need. His hand dips down my leggings, skimming the top of my panties. I let out a moan. I press up on my toes, deepening the kiss.

He picks me up, placing me on the island. I lean back on my forearms, watching him pull my pants off.

"Mmm, I feel like dessert first." He pulls my thong down, kissing the inside of my right leg all the way up. His tongue dips between my slit. "Tastes like heaven."

My hips rock forward, needing him more, and he sucks my clit hard. "Dorian," I gasp. He dips his tongue inside, grabs my hips, and pulls me closer to his face. His tongue fucking me when his finger finds my clit.

"Fuck, you taste so sweet. Come for me." He dips his finger deep inside, swiping my g-spot. When he presses harder on my clit, my legs shake. My lower stomach cramps.

"I'm coming, oh fuck." He pumps harder, and I scream as I find my release, soaking Dorian's shirt as I do.

"God, that's so hot." He stares down at his wet shirt. I cover my face. I'll never get used to squirting. "It's nothing to be embarrassed about. I love it when you come all over my face. I love you." He kisses me deep, tasting myself on his lips.

"When's fuckin' supper?" Nyx calls out before walking in. "Well, I see what dessert is." He chuckles when he sees me on the island.

Dorian helps me off the island. I grab my pants and walk to the bathroom. These men are going to make me lose my goddamn mind. They are all so intense, and it's unreal that this is my life. Today has been too much for me. Tears roll down my cheeks before I reach the bathroom.

"Get your shit together, Catalina Wilson. You're stronger than that family." I remind myself as I sit on the toilet seat lid. Propping my head in my hands. I take a couple of deep breaths.

"Come here, Catalina. Daddy has a gift for you, but you can't tell Mommy."

I smile so brightly at him that I come running across the living room. I never get gifts. Mother takes them and breaks them in front of me if I do. She tells me naughty girls don't deserve them. I've been trying to be good all week, to stay on her good side. I don't want any more beatings. Daddy pats the seat next to him on the couch.

"I know I haven't been a very good Daddy. It's hard some-times. Not everyone is strong, but we must try our best. Remember that, okay?"

"You're silly, Daddy. Where's my gift?" I'm bouncing up and down with so much excitement.

He laughs and roughs up my hair. "Here, sweety, happy birthday."

He passes me a bright pink-wrapped box. My fingers itch to unwrap it. I'm so nervous that we're going to get caught. I can only stare at it. He nudges my shoulder, encouraging me to open it. I finally tear the paper, revealing a beautiful baby doll. Tears pool in my eyes.

"Thank you, Daddy. I'll cherish her forever. Love you."

"Love you too."

Those were the last precious moments I ever shared with my dad. After my sixth birthday, he turned into a shell. I hid that baby in the floorboards in my room so she wouldn't find it. To this day, that baby is sitting on a shelf in my apartment. I don't want to wish evil on anyone, but why couldn't it be my mother who died? Why did my dad have to stay with her? Why couldn't he just leave her? There are so many questions that I don't think I'll ever get an answer to. A gentle knock pulls me out of my past.

Before I can brush the tears away, Cole opens the door. I sniffle hard when he looks at me. In two big steps, he's pulling me into his chest. Without words, he's rubbing my back, pouring his strength into me.

"Everything will be okay, baby," he whispered.

I nod into his chest. "I know, it just hit me out of nowhere, that's all."

"Did you want another minute alone?" He tilts my chin up. Taking in my face.

"No, I'm good. I'm sure Dorian has supper ready by now, anyway."

He sends me a small smirk. "I'm sure he's full of his dessert."

I smack him on the chest. "You're only jealous because he got it first."

He growls low. "Not going to lie, I totally am. But I'm going to enjoy it later when I get the entire thing." He smacks me on the ass when I turn. I let out a laugh.

"So confident of yourself." I sass back.

He lifts me over his shoulder, hauling me out of the bathroom. I smack his ass only to get one in return.

"Put me down, asshole." I squeal when he tickles my side.

"Look what I found, guys," he hollers, entering the kitchen.

They let out cheers. "I always loved my meals to go," Nyx said.

I struggle to talk with all the blood rushing to my head, and I push up on Cole's tight ass. "You're not funny, Nyx. Put me down, Cole."

He places me on my feet, holding me still. When I face the table, it's done up fancy like. They even found a white tablecloth. Black candles sit next to a bouquet in the middle of the table. This is what I needed to cheer me up, and the guys always know what I need before I do.

"What's all this?" I can't take my eyes off all their hard work, and it's gorgeous.

Dorian clears his throat. "We wanted to take you out on a date tonight." He doesn't finish his sentence; I can figure out why. It's been a lot to take in today.

"Thank you, this is really lovely." Nyx reaches his hand out for me. I take it as he guides me to my seat. I give him a smile. He winks at me as he flicks my napkin, then lays it across my lap. "Such a gentleman."

He chuckles. "For now, baby." He kisses my cheek, stepping back.

Dorian steps forward, placing my plate in front of me. I close my eyes, inhaling the aroma of the hamburger and rosemary fries. My mouth instantly waters. "Oh, Dorian, this looks amazing. Why didn't you go to culinary school instead?"

"I, school isn't for me. Enjoy half pint." He kisses me on the nose.

Cole places a glass of beer in front of me, and I side-eye him. "How did you know I don't like wine?"

"I had a feeling you weren't into that shit. Who enjoys drinking fermented fruit?"

I burst out laughing. "I couldn't agree more. Give me a barley sandwich any day of the week."

He kisses me on the lips. "That's my girl. Now eat."

They all sit with their food and beer. As we eat and chat, I think about how this room is filled with love. This entire house is filled with love. It's everything I've always wanted.

"I love you guys."

All three of them look at me with so much love they don't even need to say it.

13

NYX

What a crazy week it's been. It's the first week of December, and we're on our way to the lawyer who reached out to us. We let Cat's brother know not to communicate with her. Just trying to keep her family at a distance. I understand where she's coming from, but isn't she interested at all in what her dad had to say?

"I'm so nervous. I've never talked to a lawyer before." She straightens her black dress for the hundredth time this morning.

I grab her hands. "You'll do great. I'm here. Cole and Dorian are here. We have your back."

We all step into the office, never letting her do this alone. She'll never be alone. The look on the lawyer's face when he calls for her and we all stand is very priceless. The best part is she doesn't give a shit, and she doesn't care what others think. That's what I love about her. She does what society doesn't expect. Who says you can't share one girl with your best friends? I'll never have to worry about either of us getting jealous of each other. We'll treat her with the utmost respect, especially Cole. He's finally got it. I can see him now, hand in hand, strolling down the narrow hallway. He's not going to mess this up again.

"Please have a seat. This won't take long. I was informed of what we would be doing." The lawyer gestures to the seats across from his desk.

Dorian pulls a chair out for Cat while we remain standing. We're only here for moral support.

"I'm very sorry for your loss, Catalina. As you are aware, your father did leave you as his only beneficiary. I also know you want to turn everything over to your older brother, correct?"

"Yes, that's right. I don't want to know what he left me."

The lawyer adjusts in his seat. "Are you sure?"

She smooths her dress again. "Yes, if I'm not keeping it, it doesn't matter to me now, does it? Please, I'd rather just get this done with."

He nods and goes through the stack of paper. "If you don't mind reading over this one, it tells you we are transferring beneficiaries between you and your brother. You won't be able to come back to claim anything down the road."

We all move in closer to read over her shoulder, and I place my hand on her shoulder, squeezing it gently.

When she grabs the pen, I know she's determined to finish this once and for all.

I feel so much more alive now. Is that a thing?"

We're all sitting in front of the fireplace in the den, listening to the wood crackle. We've been in here since we came home, and she told us it's her favourite room. It's easy to figure out why.

I run my hand along her thigh. "It's a thing, baby, because you make me feel alive."

She looks up at me. "I feel like it's all a dream, and it's going to go away when I wake up."

"Never. You're ours just as much as were yours," Cole said, kissing her neck. She closes her eyes when my fingers run further up her thigh.

Dorian unzips her dress, pushing it off her shoulders. She pulls her arms free, only to be pushed onto her back by Cole.

"So beautiful, you know that little one."

She bites her lower lip and moans when my fingers inch closer to her entrance. I can feel her warmth through her panties. Inviting me closer. "Let's get this dress off you. I want to see you naked."

She pushes her heels into the floor, raising her ass up. I help shimmy her dress down her hip, throwing it into the corner. I can't help but stare down at her.

"Are you wearing matching lingerie?" It's the sexiest thing ever.

"Oh, fuck little one." Cole unbuttons his pants, pulling out that pierced cock Dorian and I dared him to get done. He strokes himself. He took it a step further and acquired the pubic piercing. Cat's eyes glaze over when she sees it.

I remove her panties, dipping my finger into her core.

"Nyx, yes." She moans. Her hand grabs for Dorian, but he's already moving to her breasts. She moans again when he sucks on her tight nipple.

"What do you want, little one?" Cole asked.

She looks between all of us. "I want Dorian in my ass, Cole in my pussy, and I want Nyx in my mouth."

"Fuck, I love it when you know what you want." Dorian kisses her lips and then moves toward the desk. When Dorian comes back, he's naked and goes to lie on the floor.

"Crawl on top, face the guys." Dorian pats his stomach for her to sit on. She crawls over him, straddling him, and his cock bobs toward her wet pussy. He grips her ass cheeks. "Mmm, this fuckin ass of yours. I can't wait to be deep inside of it." Her hips rock forward.

Her fingers dip down to her clit, moaning as she circles her bud. I unzip my jeans, stepping close to her.

"Are you ready for all of us, baby?"

"Mm, yeah. Please, I need you all."

Dorian hands her the bottle of lube, and she takes it, squirting some on his cock. Cole kneels between Dorian's legs, stroking himself. He pushes her onto Dorian's chest, taking the lube from her. Pressing a finger into her tight hole, she lets out a hiss. Her small hand wraps around my shaft, pulling my eyes away from the show. I close my eyes, tilting my head back. The sound of her moans pulls me back. Dorian is pressing into her ass while Cole eats her out.

"Fuck, this is everything. Look at you. Take all your men." I wrap my hand around her hair, pulling her face towards my cock. She licks her lips, opening wide for me. I groan when she sucks me hard. The vibration of her moans causes me to thrust further into her mouth. "Oh, shit, baby." I look down and see that Dorian and Cole are moving inside her, giving her the pleasure she needs.

"Such a good girl, aren't you, little one?" Cole pulls her hips closer to him.

She mumbles around my cock. "I'm gonna come soon." I push deeper into her mouth until she gags, and tears appear in her eyes. My balls tighten, and my body tingles. I thrust faster, throwing my head back, and I come down her throat. Slowing down, she swallows around my cock before I pull out. "Fuck, I love you." I give her a deep kiss before I sit down.

I watch the three of them; they move with each other, paying attention to each other's different needs. It's a beautiful sight. She screams, her release slumping more into Dorian's chest. Her black hair fanning out on his chest. Dorian lets out a loud groan, going still. His eyes are closed. Cole is quick to follow, leaning forward and kissing her chest.

The entire den is filled with heavy breathing, and Cat's eyes are closing from exhaustion. I pull my pants on, heading upstairs to Cole's room. He's the one with the nice bathtub. I turn the water on and head into his bathroom to grab a towel. I set everything up for her before I head back downstairs.

"All right, baby girl. I have a nice bath running for you. Let's get that nice ass of yours upstairs."

Her eyes light up. "In Cole's room?"

"Yes, that one."

She quickly gets up, dancing around with excitement. "I've been dying to get into the one."

"You never have to ask. It's there for your use anytime," Cole says.

She jumps into his arms. "Love you."

He narrows his eyes. "Me or the tub?"

She taps her chin; he tickles her side, getting a high-pitched squeal from her.

"Come before the water overflows."

I carry her up the stairs with her head on my shoulder. "Thank you, Nyx."

"Anything for you, baby."

It's a boring night. Cat had to work again, which I can't complain about. She's getting out of her shell. Working with another human will do her good. Despite what she told me about Riley, he doesn't talk much. Then again, she's not outside in the cold until spring. I will never dig up a dead body, give me a gun, and let me shoot someone any day of the week instead. I don't have to look them in the eyes afterward. Just thinking about touching a stiff body turns my stomach.

I'm sitting at home when my phone rings.

"Hey, what's up?"

"I'm gonna pick Cat up from work tonight. Can you bring the supplies and meet us in the cemetery?"

"Does Dorian know the plan, or did you want me to fill him in?"

Cole chuckled. "He knows. He's excited."

Of course, he is. "All right, I'll meet you guys there."

This is one surprise Catalina won't forget, and there are some things we would like to do to remind her of our beginnings.

Dorian and I are waiting for Cole and Catalina to show up in the far corner of the cemetery. My heart rate picks up as soon as we see those lights flicker across the tombstones.

"Cole, what are we doing here? It's cold and late." Her soft voice carries across the quiet night. I left Cole's surprise where he wanted it.

Dorian and I make our way toward them, her back facing away from us. She must hear the leaves crunch under our shoes because she swivels around. Her face breaks into a slow smile when she notices us.

"What do you say, baby? Wanna play a game?"

She bites her lip. "Yes, please, green." She drops the very first nickname she ever gave me.

My neon mask turned on with my green light shining in the night. Next to me is Dorian with his red mask and Cole with his blue mask behind her.

"You better start running, then, so we can catch you," Dorian told her.

She looks over her shoulder to see Cole swigging a pair of handcuffs. "Oh, fuck," she mumbles. She darts to the side, taking off fast.

We all laugh before we take off after her.

THE STORY CONTINUES...

ABOUT THE AUTHOR

Hello, loves! I'm a Canadian romance writer who's all about the steamy and dark stuff. Horror books, movies, and music? Yes, please! I have a little true crime obsession, but I'll just call it research and pretend it's normal. If you crave love stories that push the limits of lust, trust, and desire, you've come to the right place. Follow me for exclusive sneak peeks, giveaways, and behind-the-scenes glimpses into my writing process. And if you want to keep up with my latest releases or connect on social media, click the link below

Let's dive into the shadows together, darlings.

ALSO BY

A HITMAN'S DUET
MYLES

CARTER

RUSSO MAFIA SERIES
UNBROKEN

UNBEARABLE

UNDENIABLE

STRANGERS OF EASTWOOD
STRANGERS OF THE NIGHT

STRANGERS OF THE TOWN

STRANGERS OF THE CROWD

RAVENWOOD ACADEMY
ATTICUS

ASHTON

MADDOX

STANDALONE
CHRISTMAS UNWRAPPED

PAINFULLY MERRY

SWEET DREAMS